D1505301

STONE ARCH BOOKS
a capstone imprint

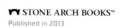

STONE ARCH BOOKS™
Published in 2013
A Capstone Imprint
1710 Roe Crest Drive
North Mankato, MN 56003
www.capstonepub.com

Originally published by DC Comics in the U.S. in single magazine form as Tiny Titans #7.

DC Comics
1700 Broadway, New York, NY 10019
A Warner Bros. Entertainment Company

Cataloging-in-Publication Data is available at the Library of Congress website:
ISBN: 978-1-4342-4698-1 (library binding)

Summary: The Tiny Titans blast through the galaxy to help their friend Starfire clean her room. Plus, more Titans fun!

STONE ARCH BOOKS
Ashley C. Andersen Zantop *Publisher*
Michael Dahl *Editorial Director*
Donald Lemke & Alison Deering *Editors*
Heather Kindseth *Creative Director*
Hilary Wacholz *Designer*
Kathy McColley *Production Specialist*

DC COMICS
Jann Jones *Original U.S. Editor*
Stephanie Buscema *U.S. Assistant Editor*

Printed in China by Nordica.
1012/CA21201277
092012 006935NORDS13

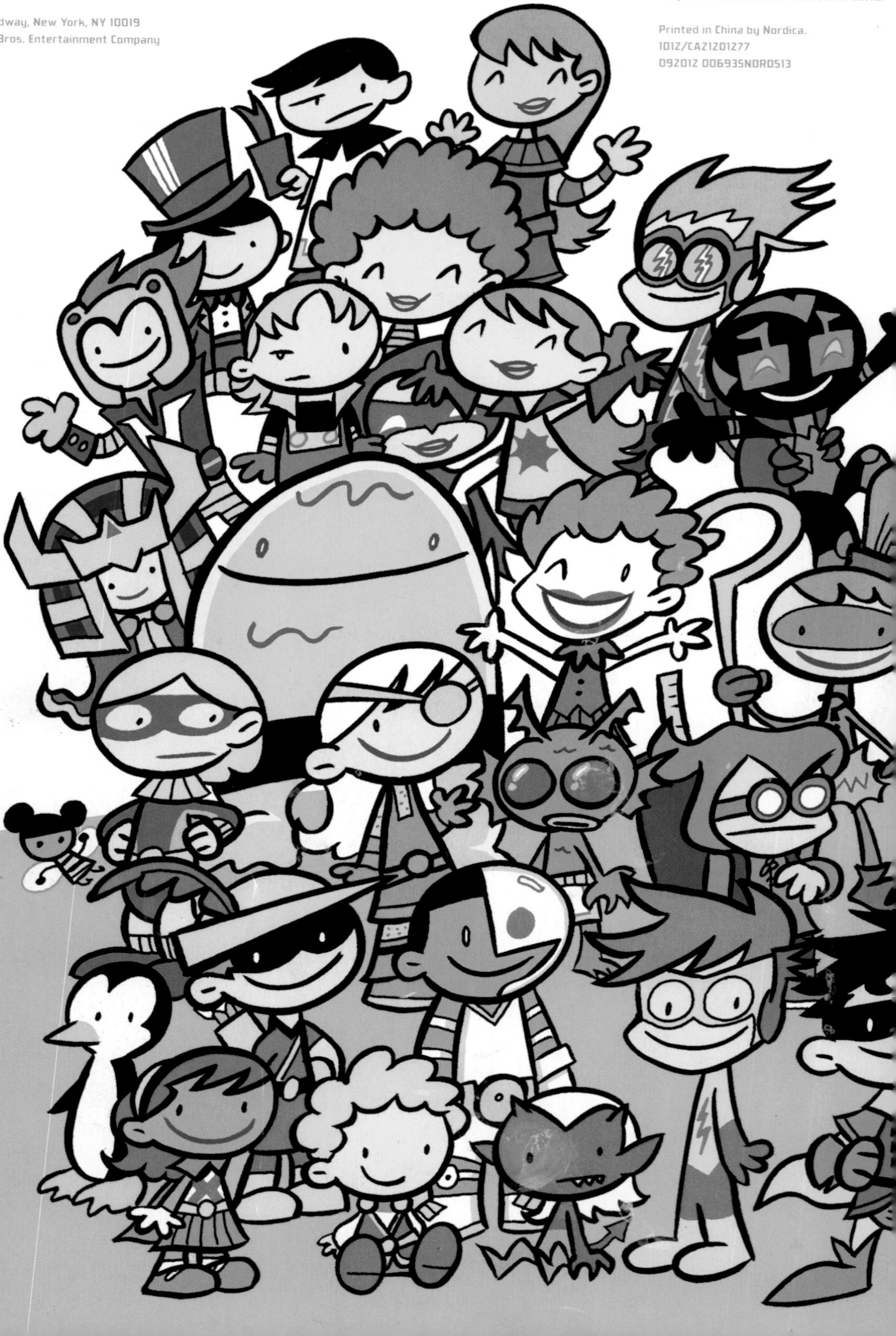

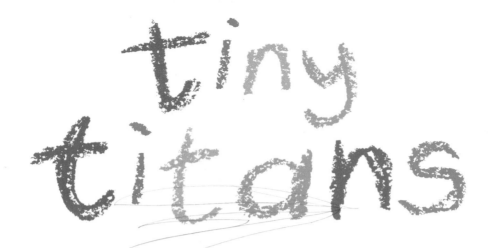

tiny titans

Titans in Space

By Eisner Winners
Art Baltazar & Franco

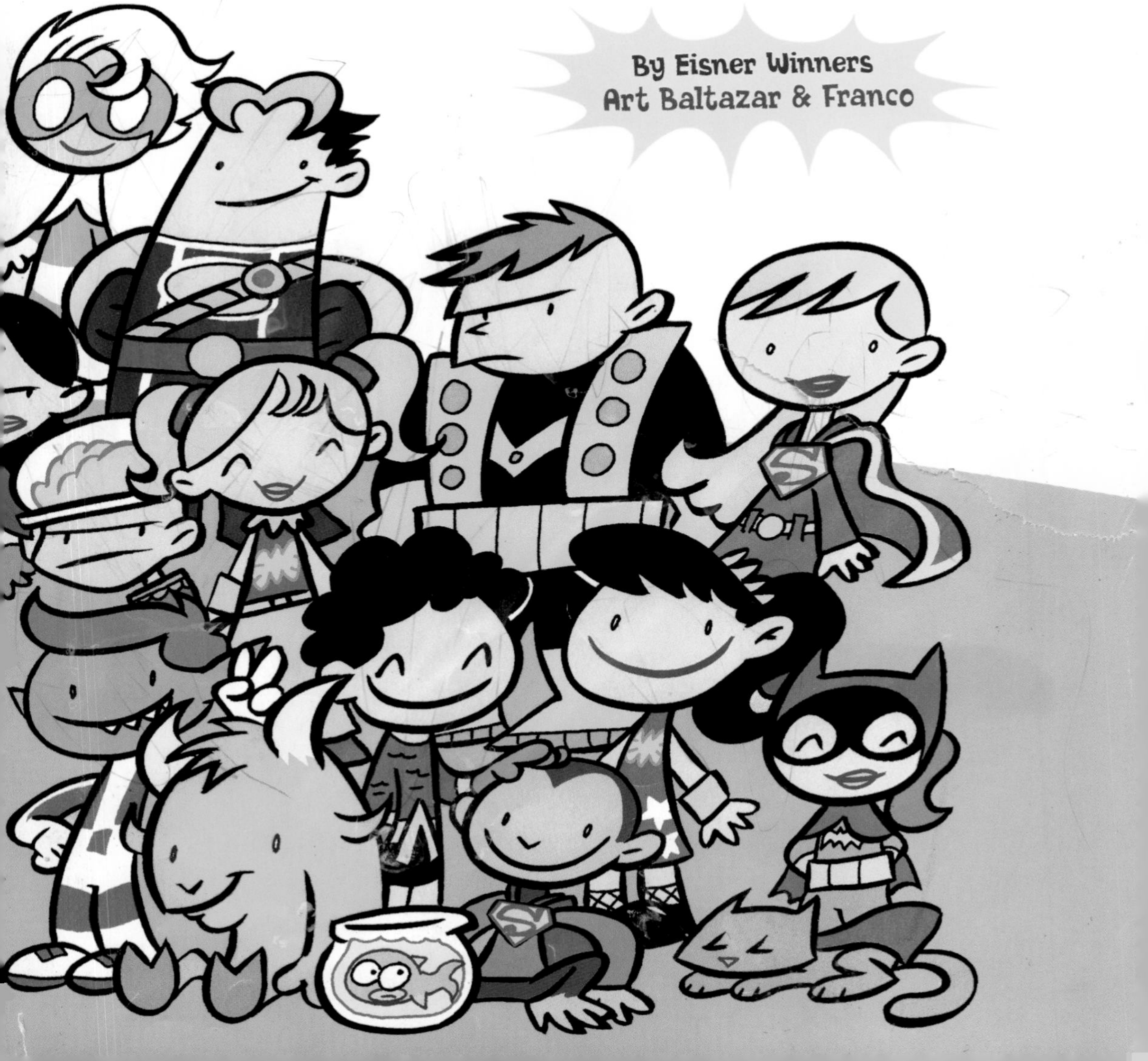

tiny titans

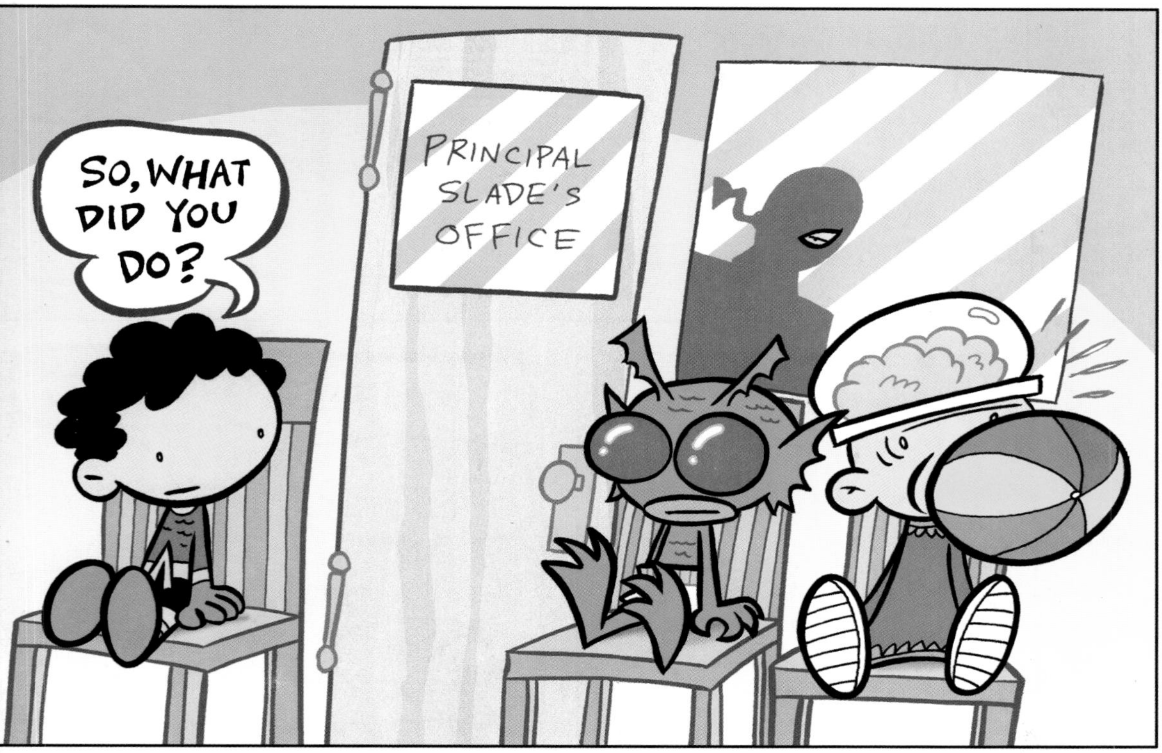
SO, WHAT DID YOU DO?
PRINCIPAL SLADE'S OFFICE

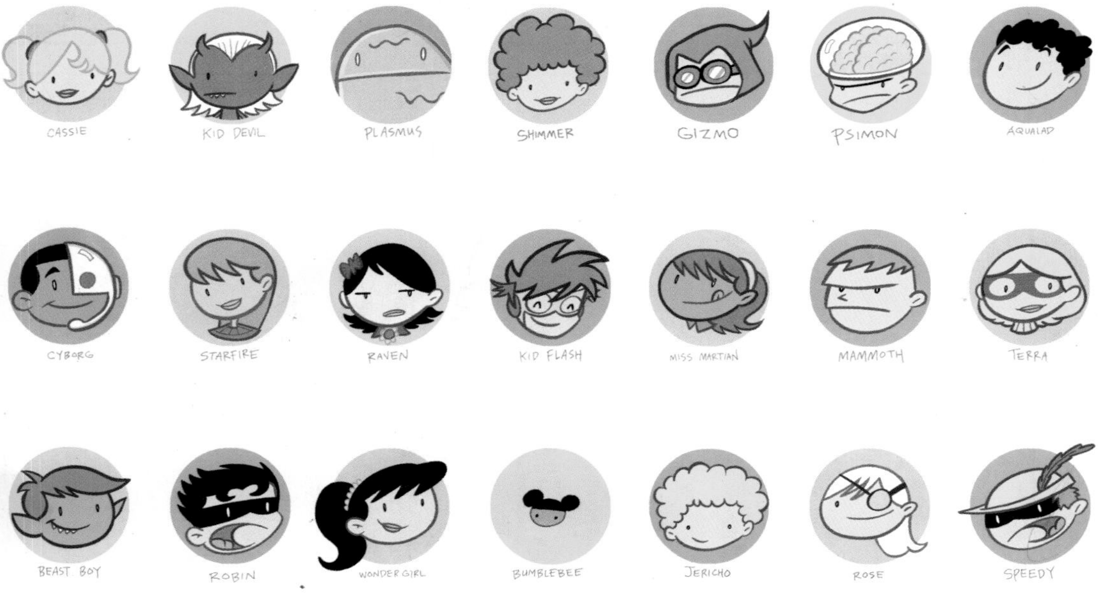
CASSIE
KID DEVIL
PLASMUS
SHIMMER
GIZMO
PSIMON
AQUALAD
CYBORG
STARFIRE
RAVEN
KID FLASH
MISS MARTIAN
MAMMOTH
TERRA
BEAST BOY
ROBIN
WONDER GIRL
BUMBLEBEE
JERICHO
ROSE
SPEEDY

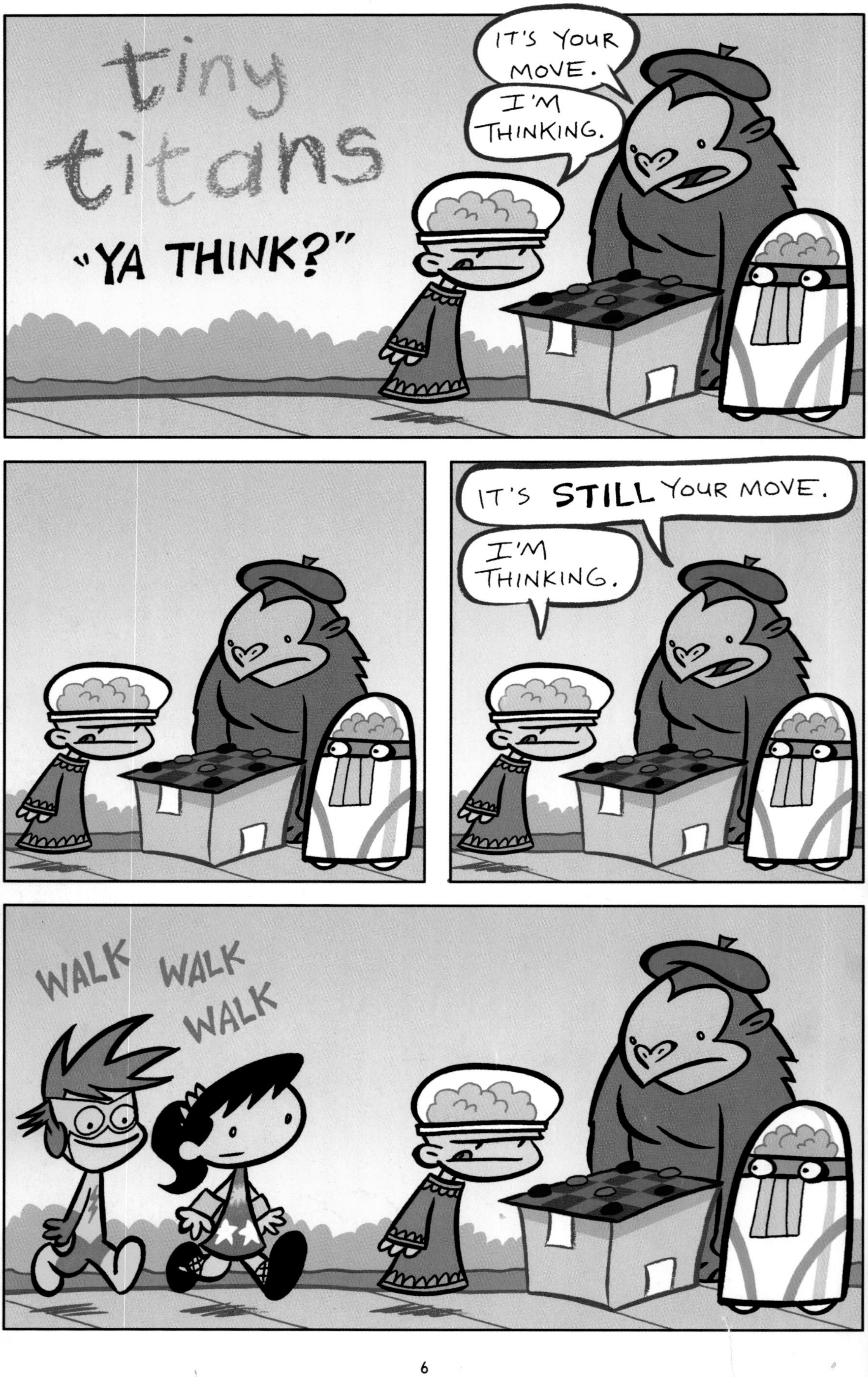
tiny titans
"YA THINK?"
IT'S YOUR MOVE.
I'M THINKING.
IT'S STILL YOUR MOVE.
I'M THINKING.
WALK
WALK
WALK
WALK

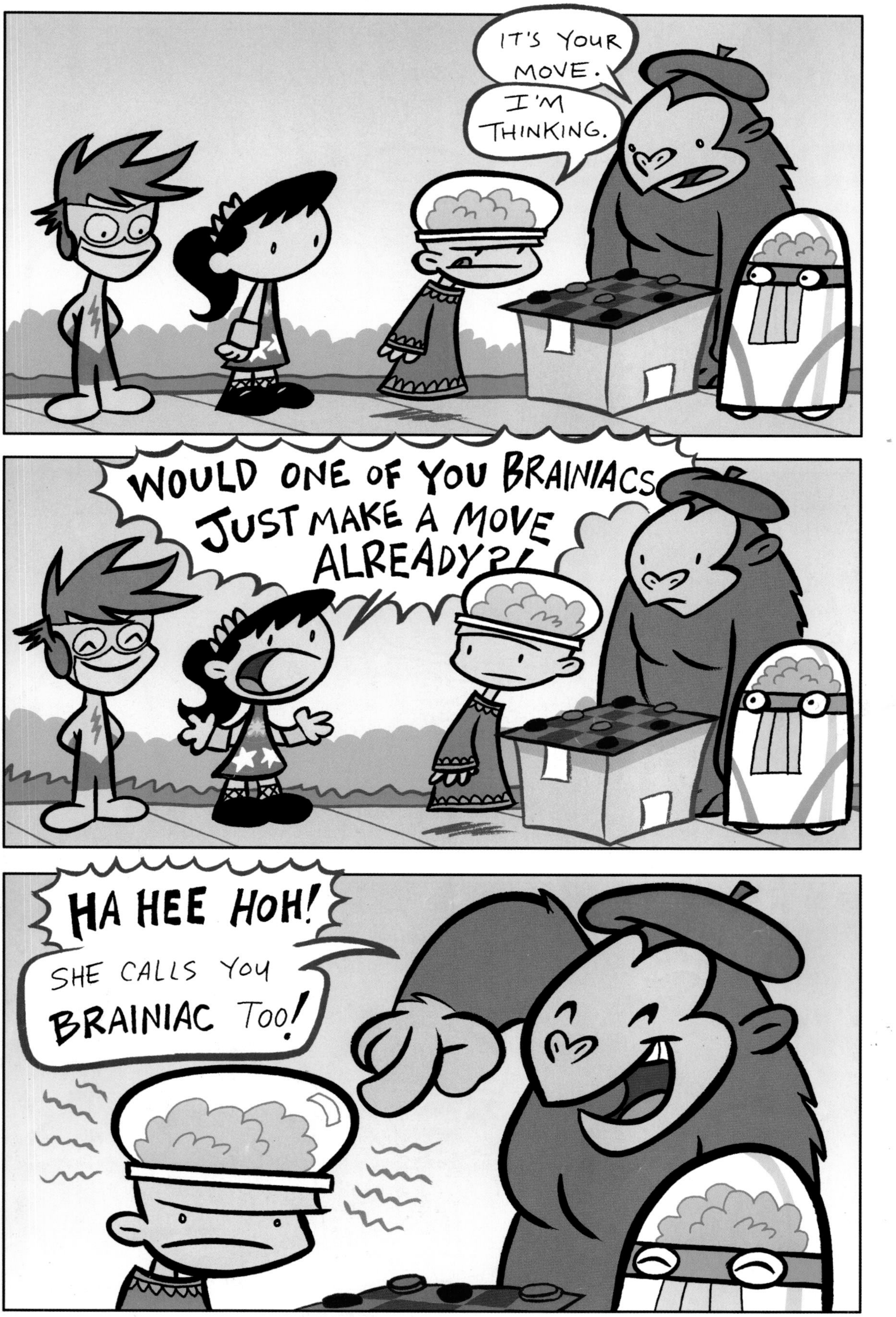
IT'S YOUR MOVE.
I'M THINKING.
WOULD ONE OF YOU BRAINIACS JUST MAKE A MOVE ALREADY?!
HA HEE HOH!
SHE CALLS YOU BRAINIAC TOO!

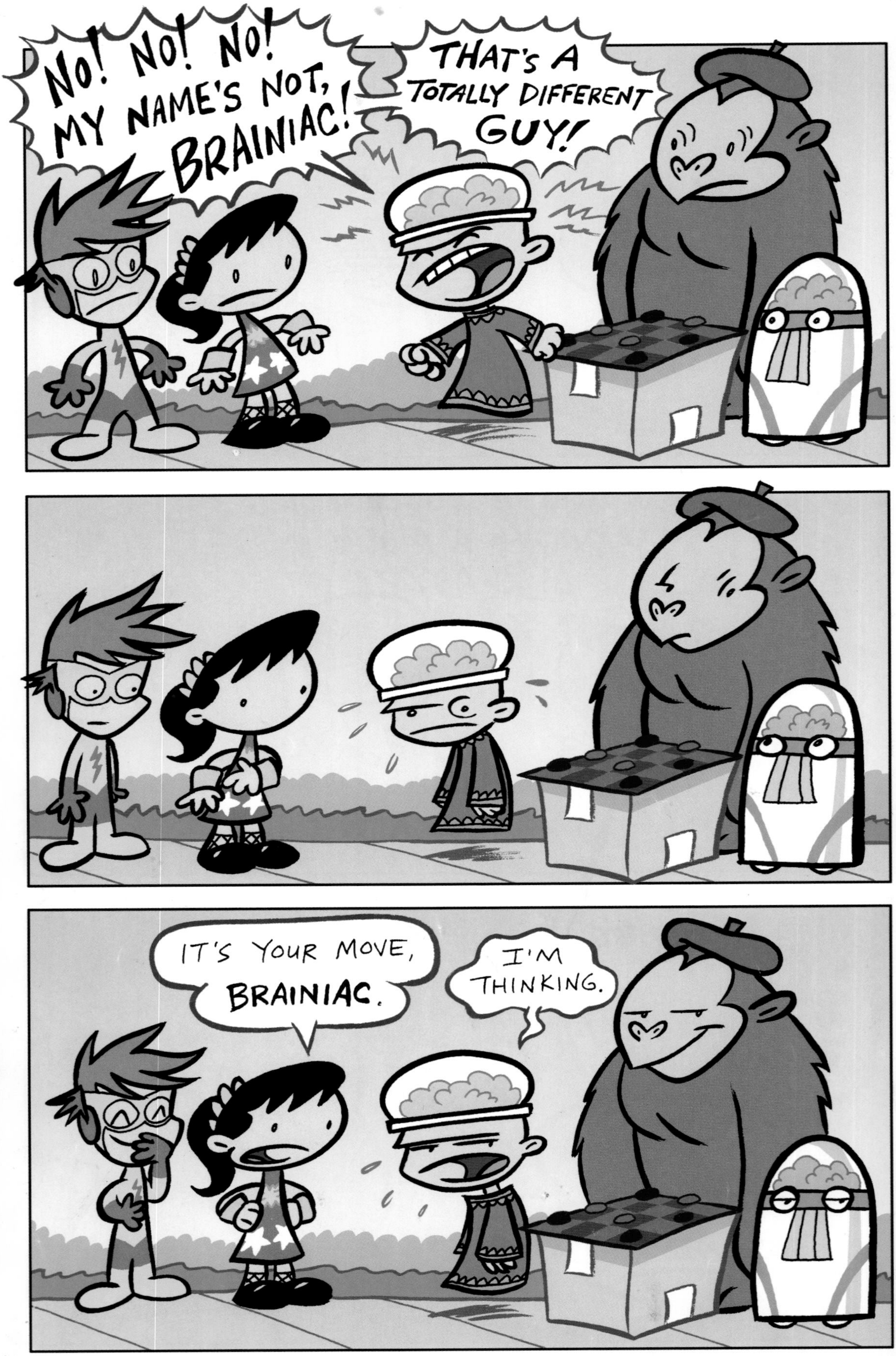
No! No! No! My name's not, Brainiac!
That's a totally different guy!
It's your move, Brainiac.
I'm thinking.

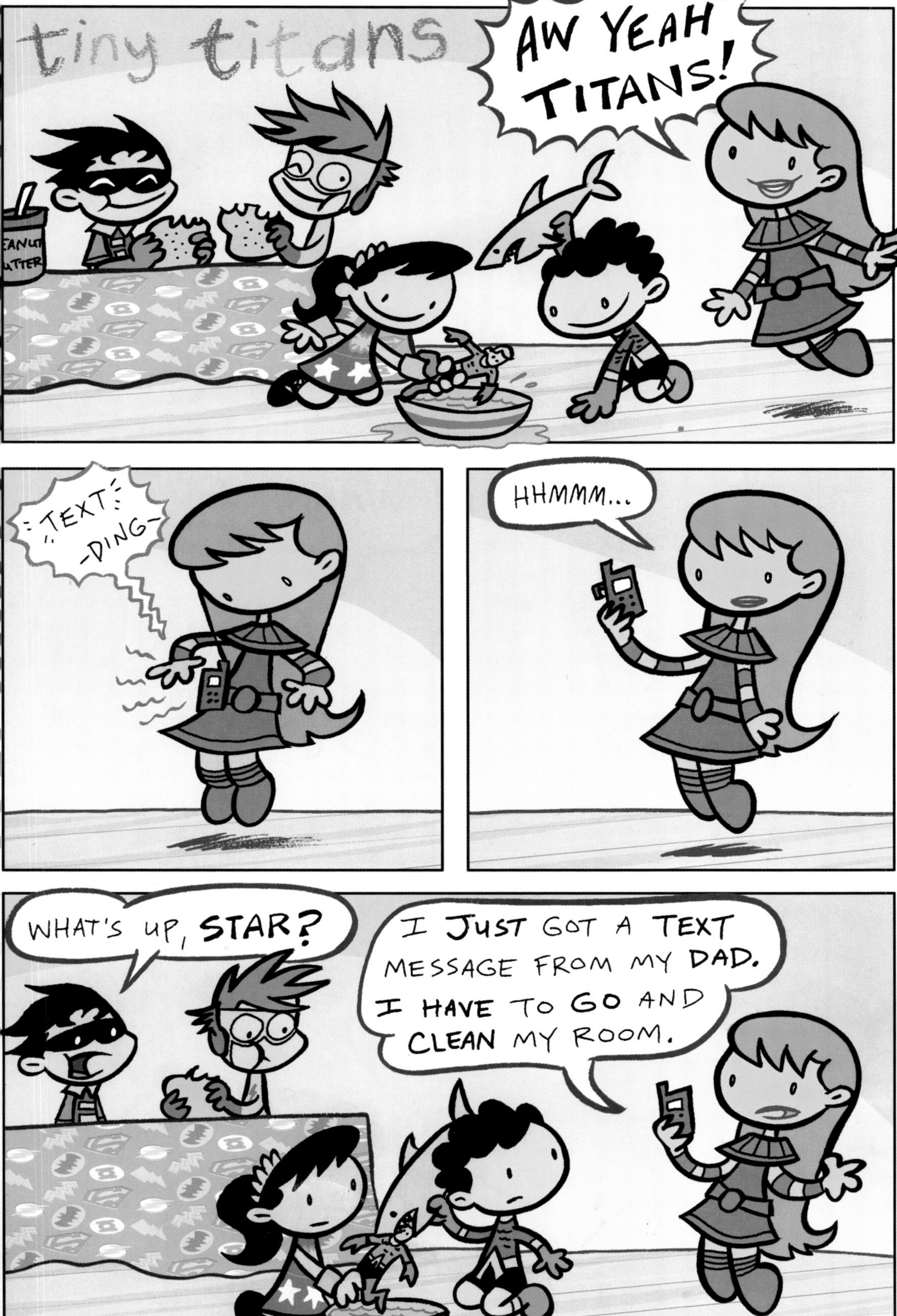
tiny titans
AW YEAH TITANS!
PEANUT BUTTER
TEXT -DING-
HHMMM...
WHAT'S UP, STAR?
I JUST GOT A TEXT MESSAGE FROM MY DAD. I HAVE TO GO AND CLEAN MY ROOM.

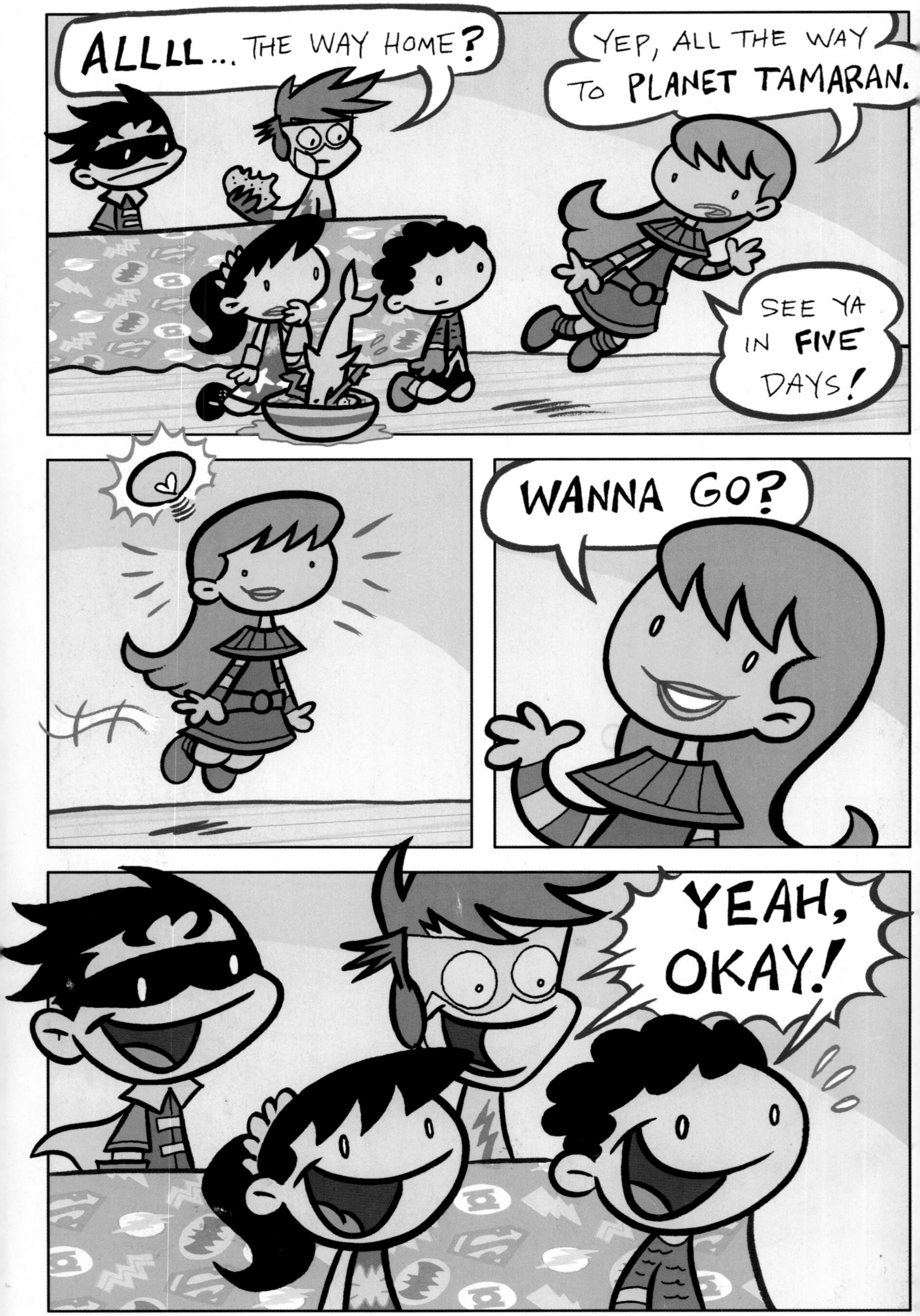
ALLLL... THE WAY HOME?
YEP, ALL THE WAY TO PLANET TAMARAN.
SEE YA IN FIVE DAYS!
WANNA GO?
YEAH, OKAY!

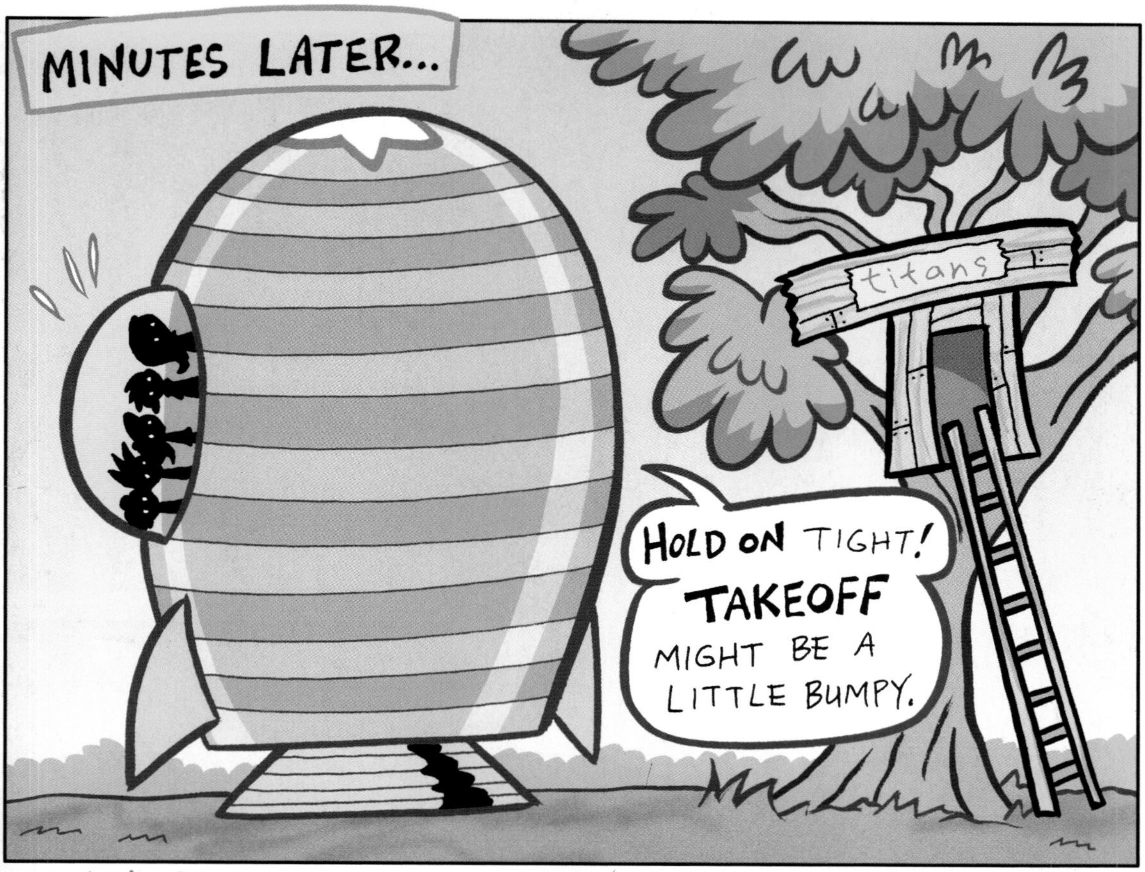
MINUTES LATER...
titans
HOLD ON TIGHT! TAKEOFF MIGHT BE A LITTLE BUMPY.

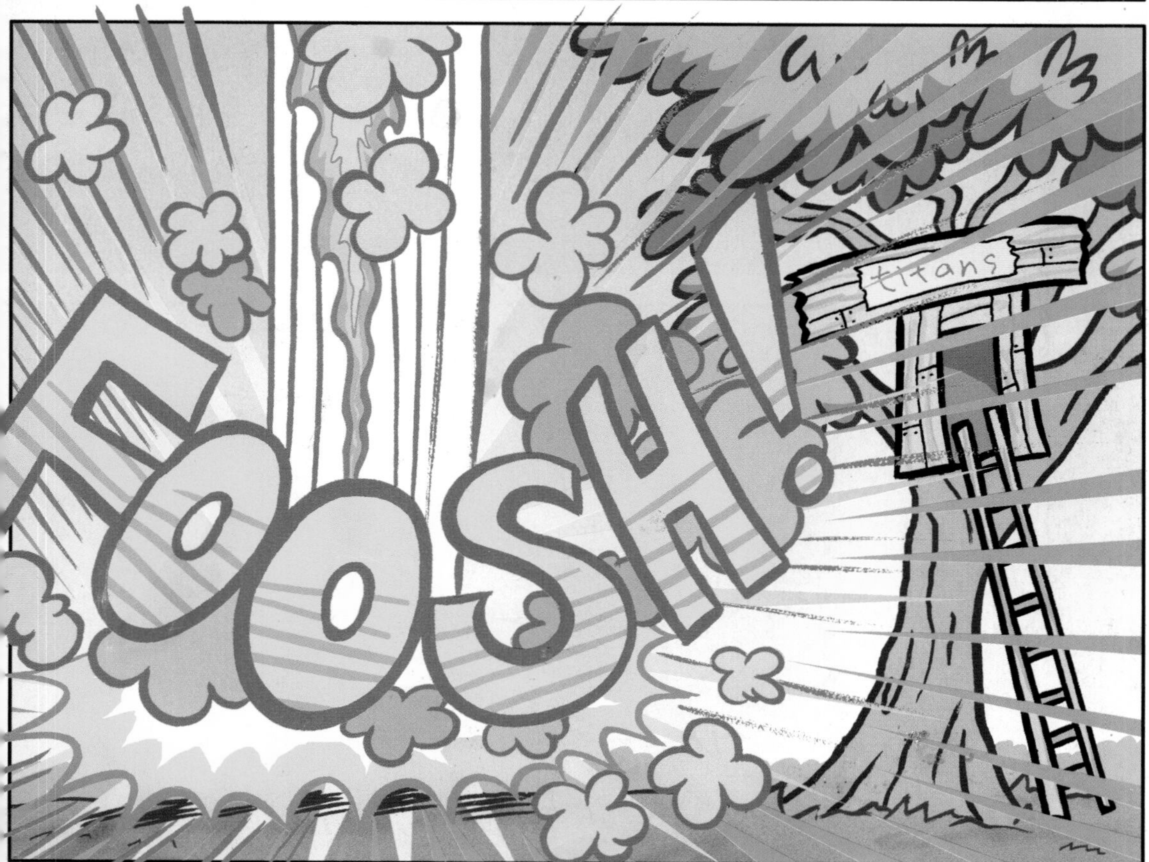
titans
FOOSH!

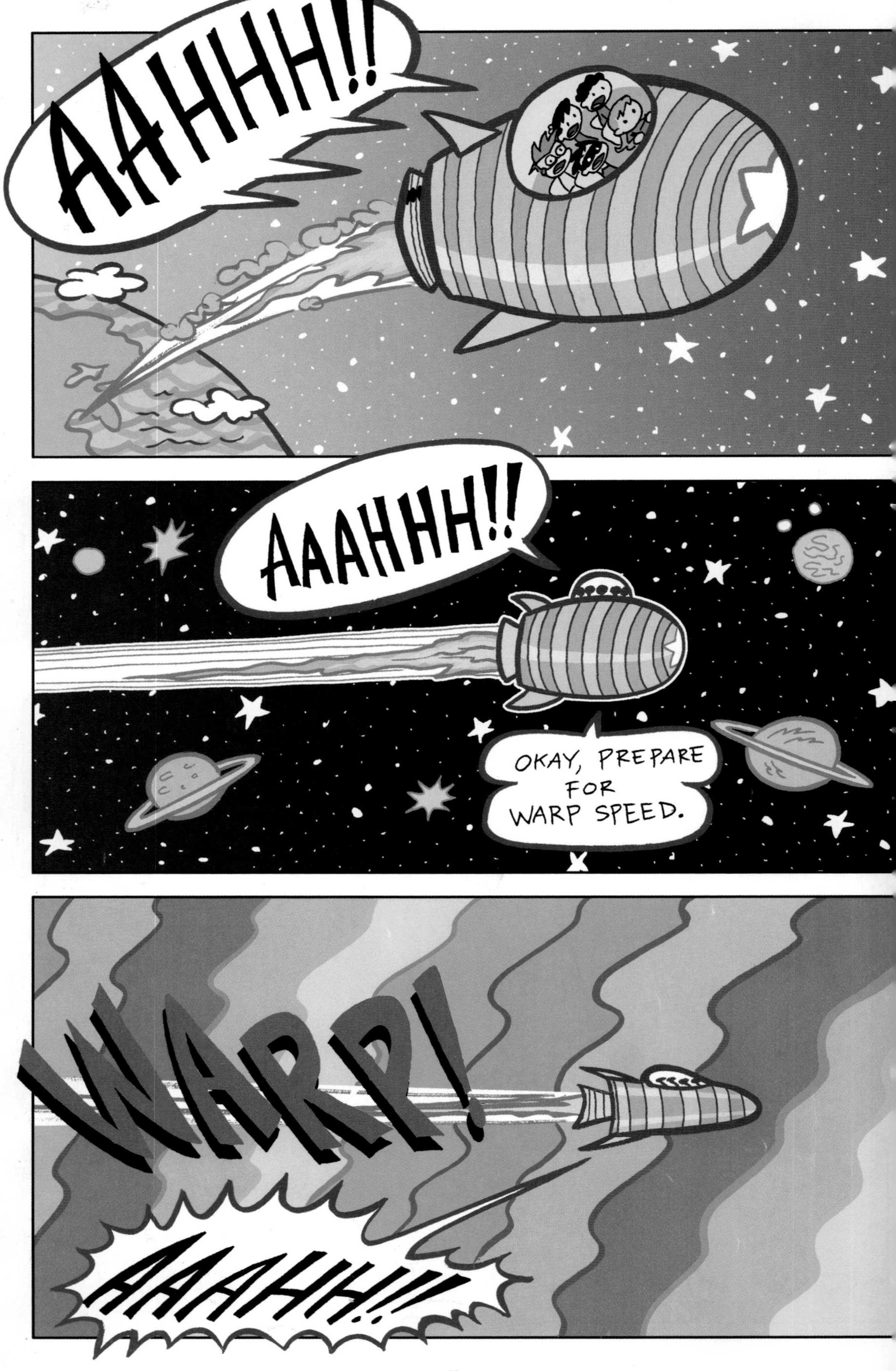
AAHHH!!
AAAHHH!!
OKAY, PREPARE FOR WARP SPEED.
WARP!
AAAHH!!

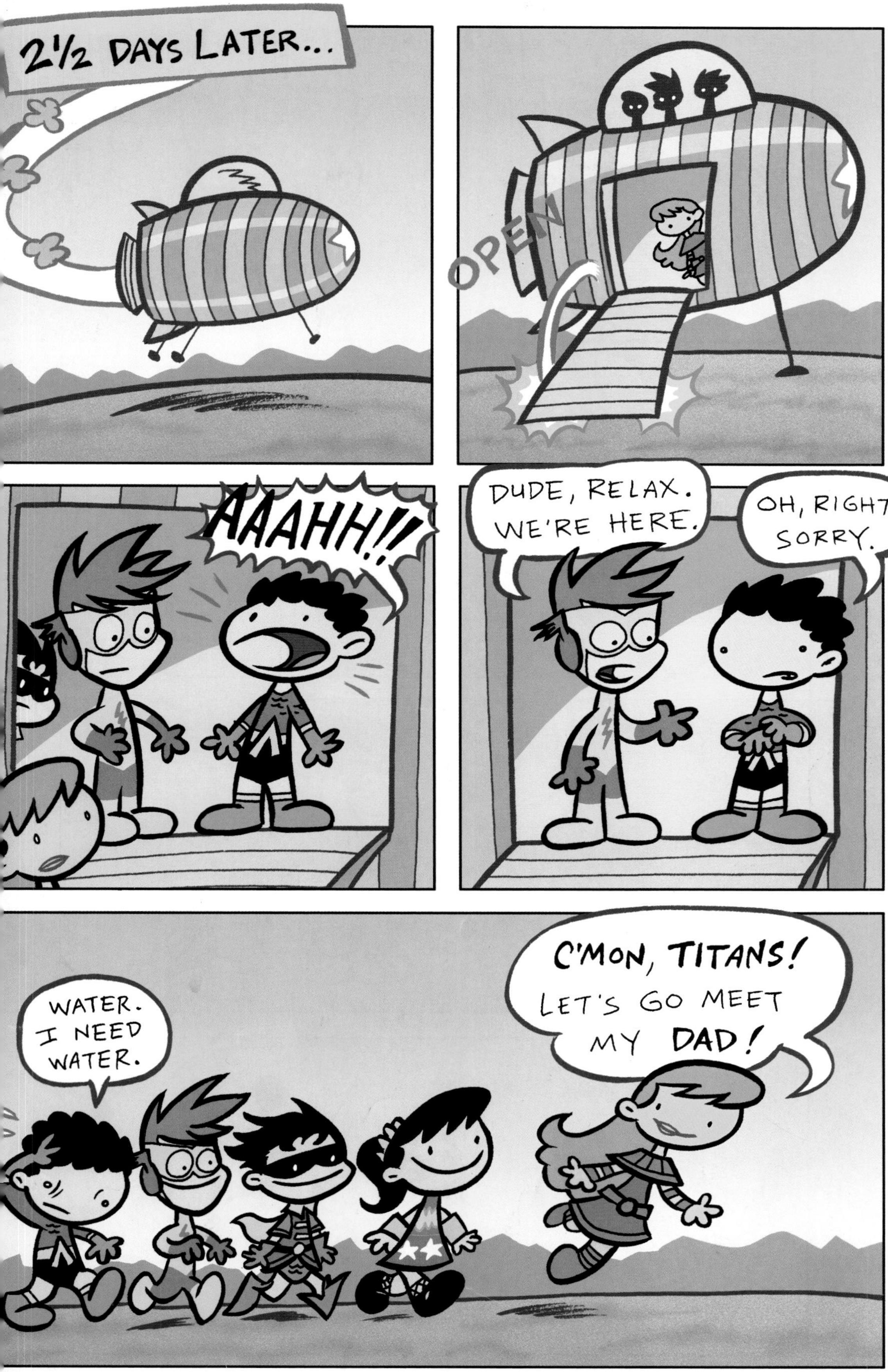
2½ DAYS LATER...
OPEN
AAAHH!!
DUDE, RELAX. WE'RE HERE.
OH, RIGHT. SORRY.
WATER. I NEED WATER.
C'MON, TITANS! LET'S GO MEET MY DAD!

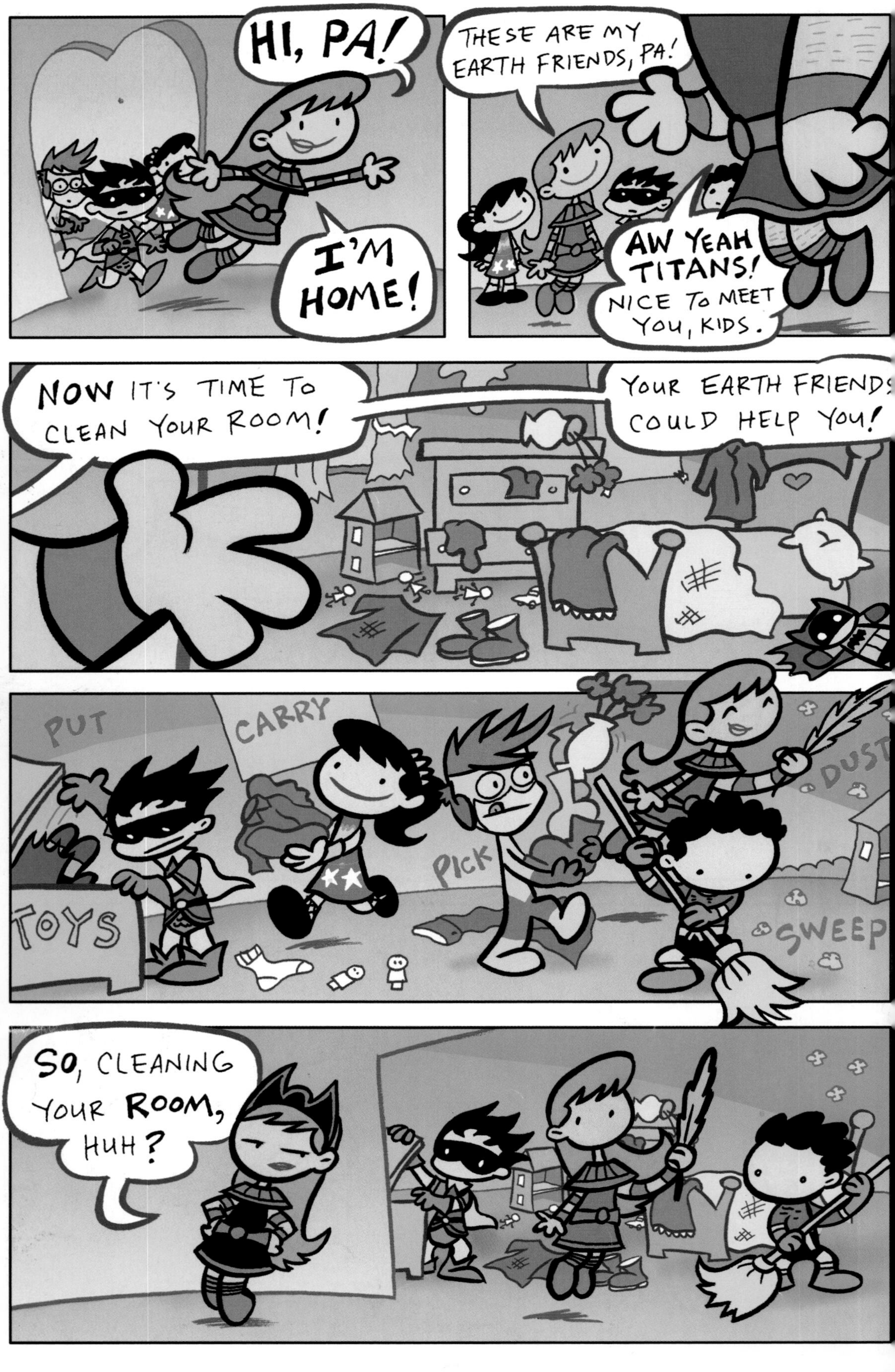
HI, PA!
I'M HOME!
THESE ARE MY EARTH FRIENDS, PA!
AW YEAH TITANS! NICE TO MEET YOU, KIDS.
NOW IT'S TIME TO CLEAN YOUR ROOM!
YOUR EARTH FRIENDS COULD HELP YOU!
PUT
CARRY
DUST
PICK
TOYS
SWEEP
SO, CLEANING YOUR ROOM, HUH?

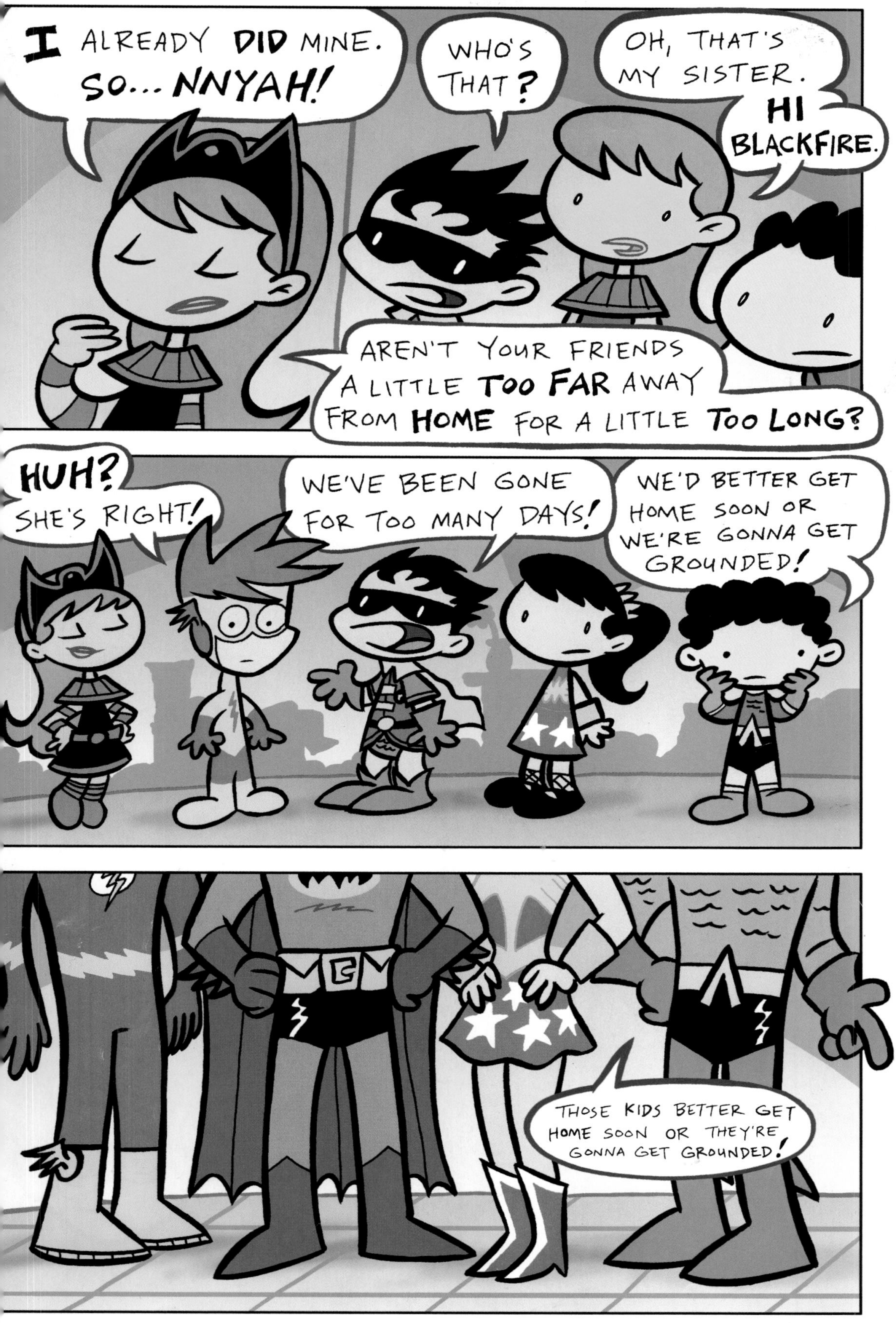
I ALREADY DID MINE. SO... NNYAH!
WHO'S THAT?
OH, THAT'S MY SISTER. HI BLACKFIRE.
AREN'T YOUR FRIENDS A LITTLE TOO FAR AWAY FROM HOME FOR A LITTLE TOO LONG?
HUH? SHE'S RIGHT!
WE'VE BEEN GONE FOR TOO MANY DAYS!
WE'D BETTER GET HOME SOON OR WE'RE GONNA GET GROUNDED!
THOSE KIDS BETTER GET HOME SOON OR THEY'RE GONNA GET GROUNDED!

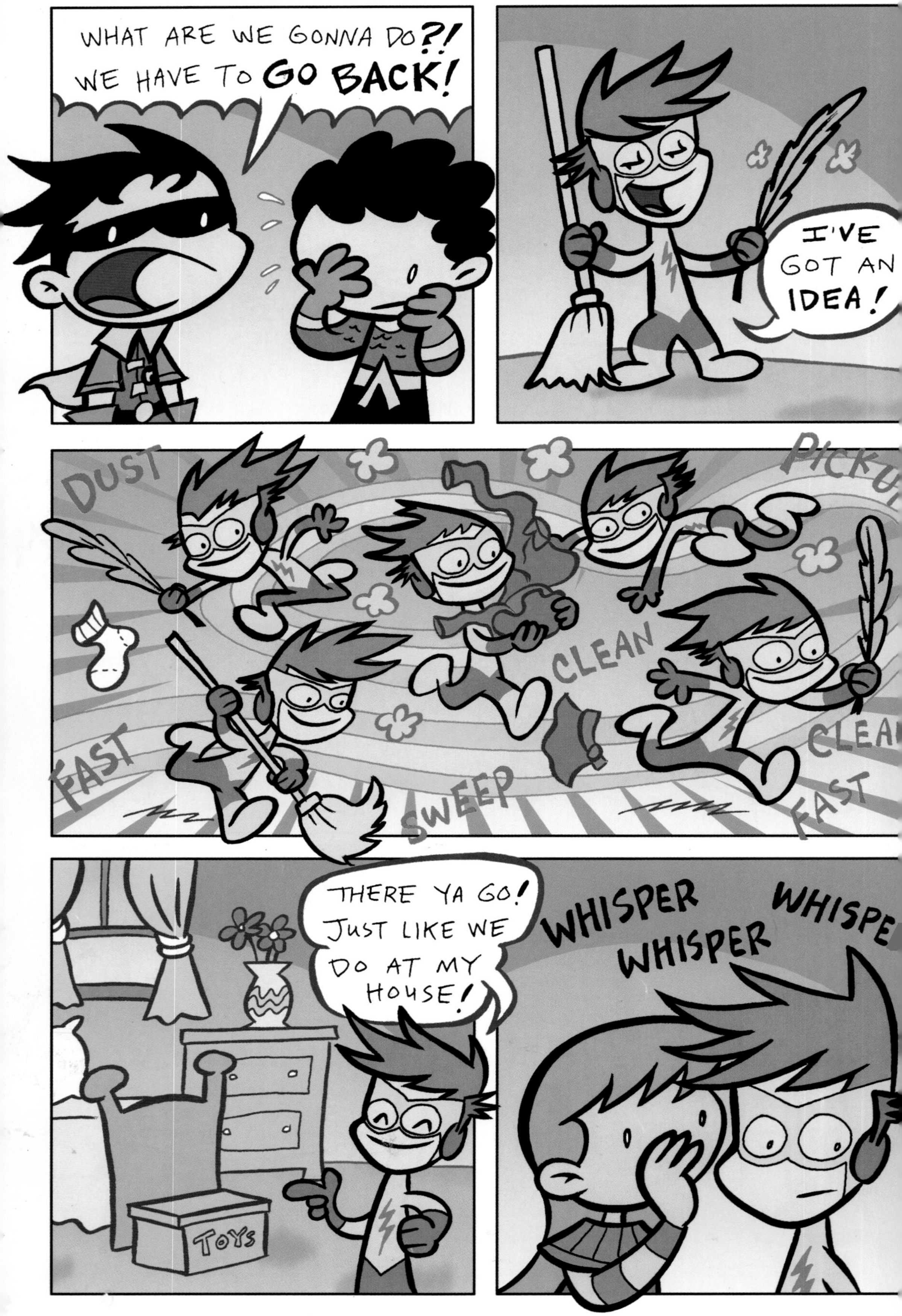
WHAT ARE WE GONNA DO?! WE HAVE TO GO BACK!
I'VE GOT AN IDEA!
DUST
PICKUP
CLEAN
FAST
SWEEP
CLEAN
FAST
THERE YA GO! JUST LIKE WE DO AT MY HOUSE!
TOYS
WHISPER
WHISPER
WHISPER

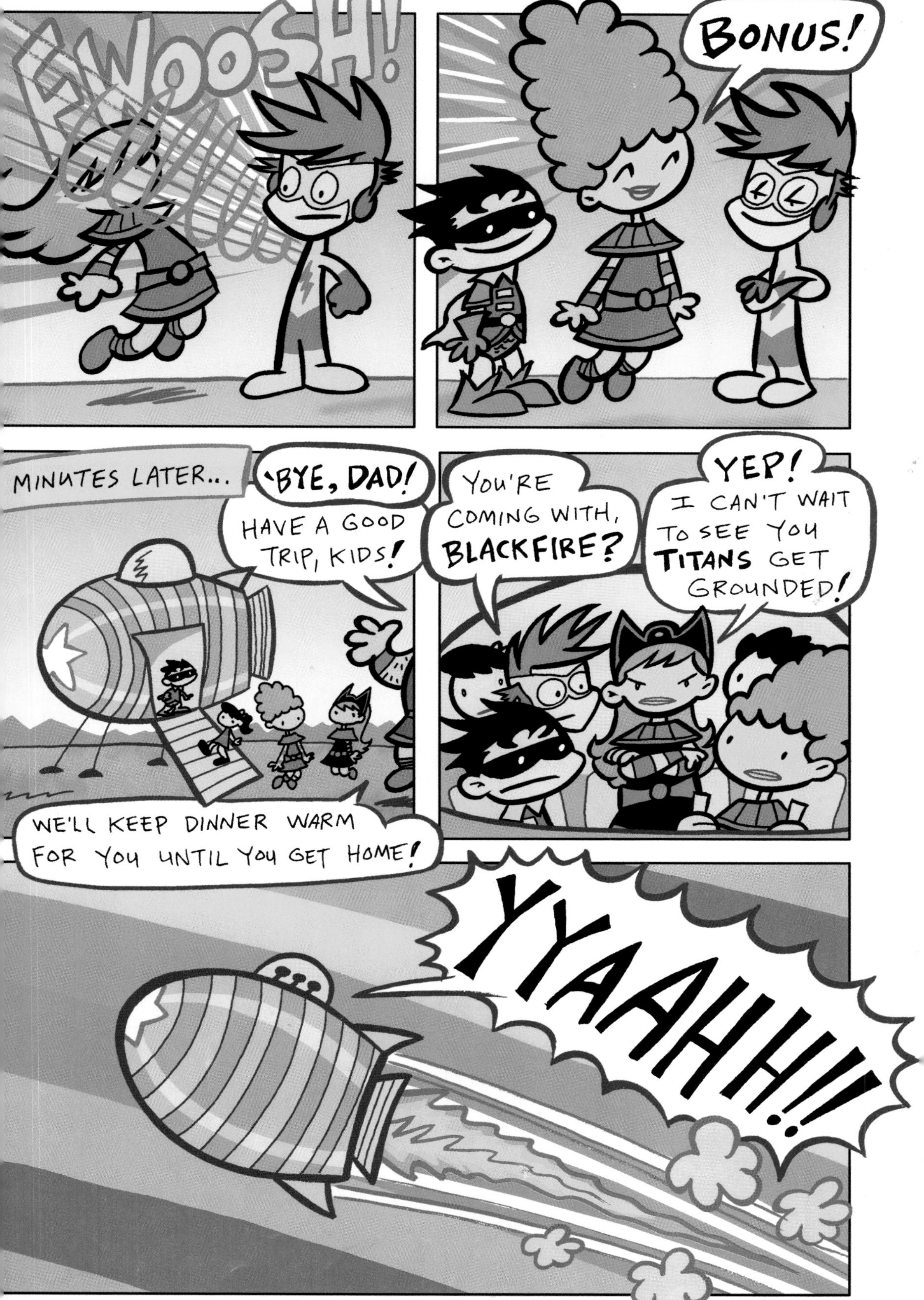
WOOSH!
BONUS!
MINUTES LATER...
'BYE, DAD!
HAVE A GOOD TRIP, KIDS!
WE'LL KEEP DINNER WARM FOR YOU UNTIL YOU GET HOME!
YOU'RE COMING WITH, BLACKFIRE?
YEP!
I CAN'T WAIT TO SEE YOU TITANS GET GROUNDED!
YYAAHH!!

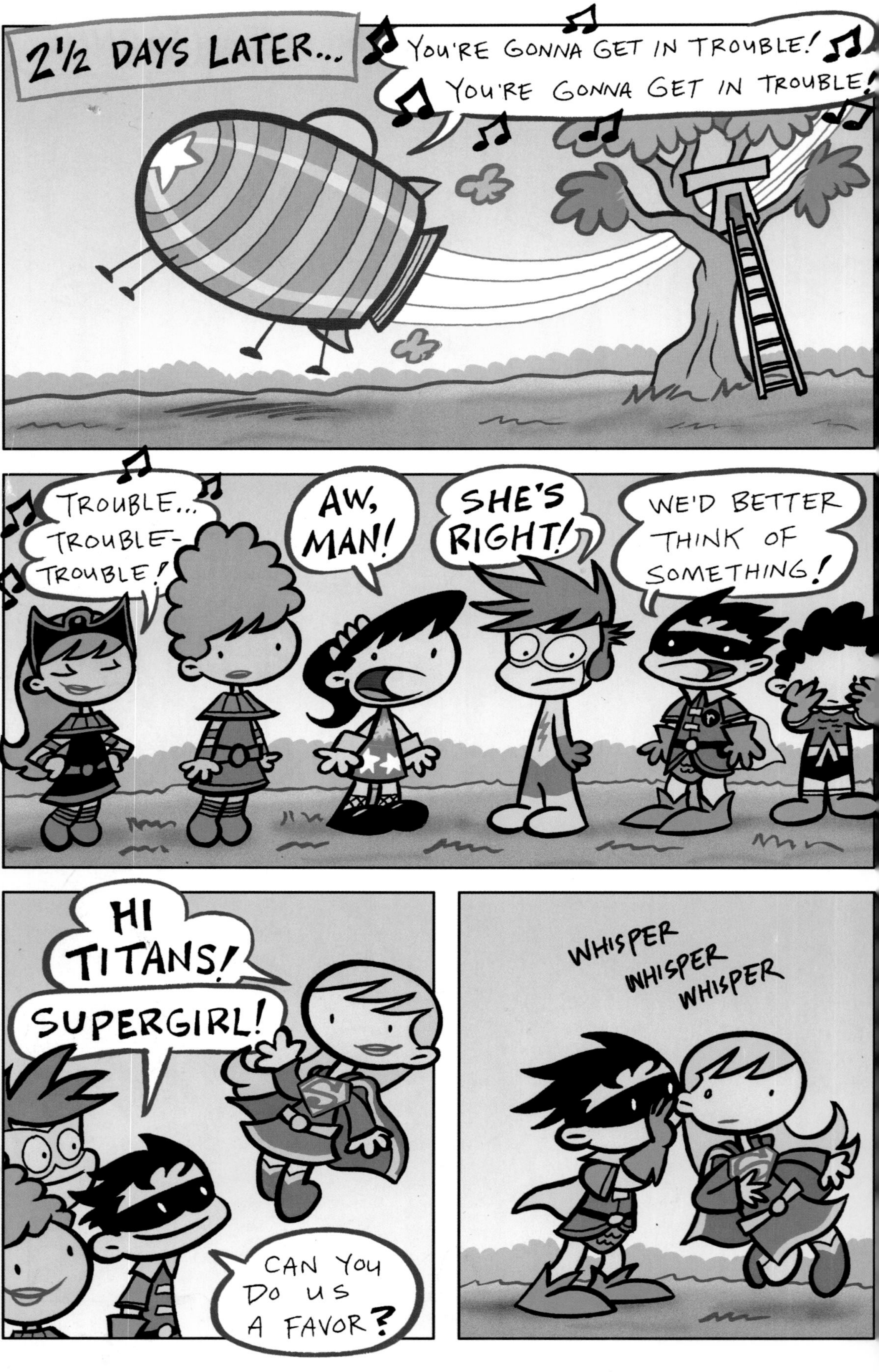
2½ DAYS LATER...
YOU'RE GONNA GET IN TROUBLE! YOU'RE GONNA GET IN TROUBLE!
TROUBLE... TROUBLE-TROUBLE!
AW, MAN!
SHE'S RIGHT!
WE'D BETTER THINK OF SOMETHING!
HI TITANS!
SUPERGIRL!
CAN YOU DO US A FAVOR?
WHISPER WHISPER WHISPER

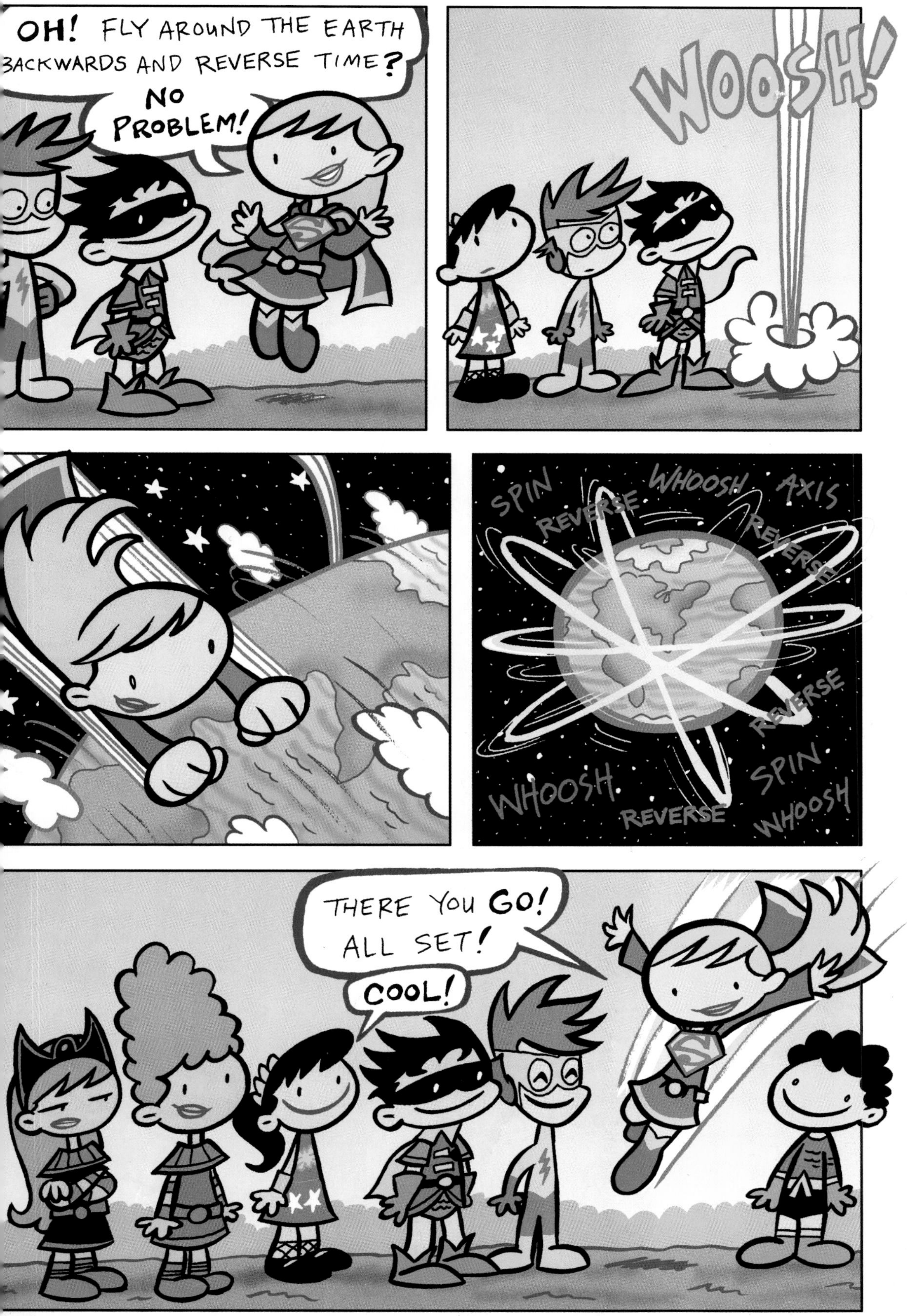
OH! FLY AROUND THE EARTH BACKWARDS AND REVERSE TIME?
NO PROBLEM!
WOOSH!
SPIN
REVERSE
WHOOSH
AXIS
REVERSE
REVERSE
SPIN
WHOOSH
REVERSE
WHOOSH
THERE YOU GO! ALL SET!
COOL!

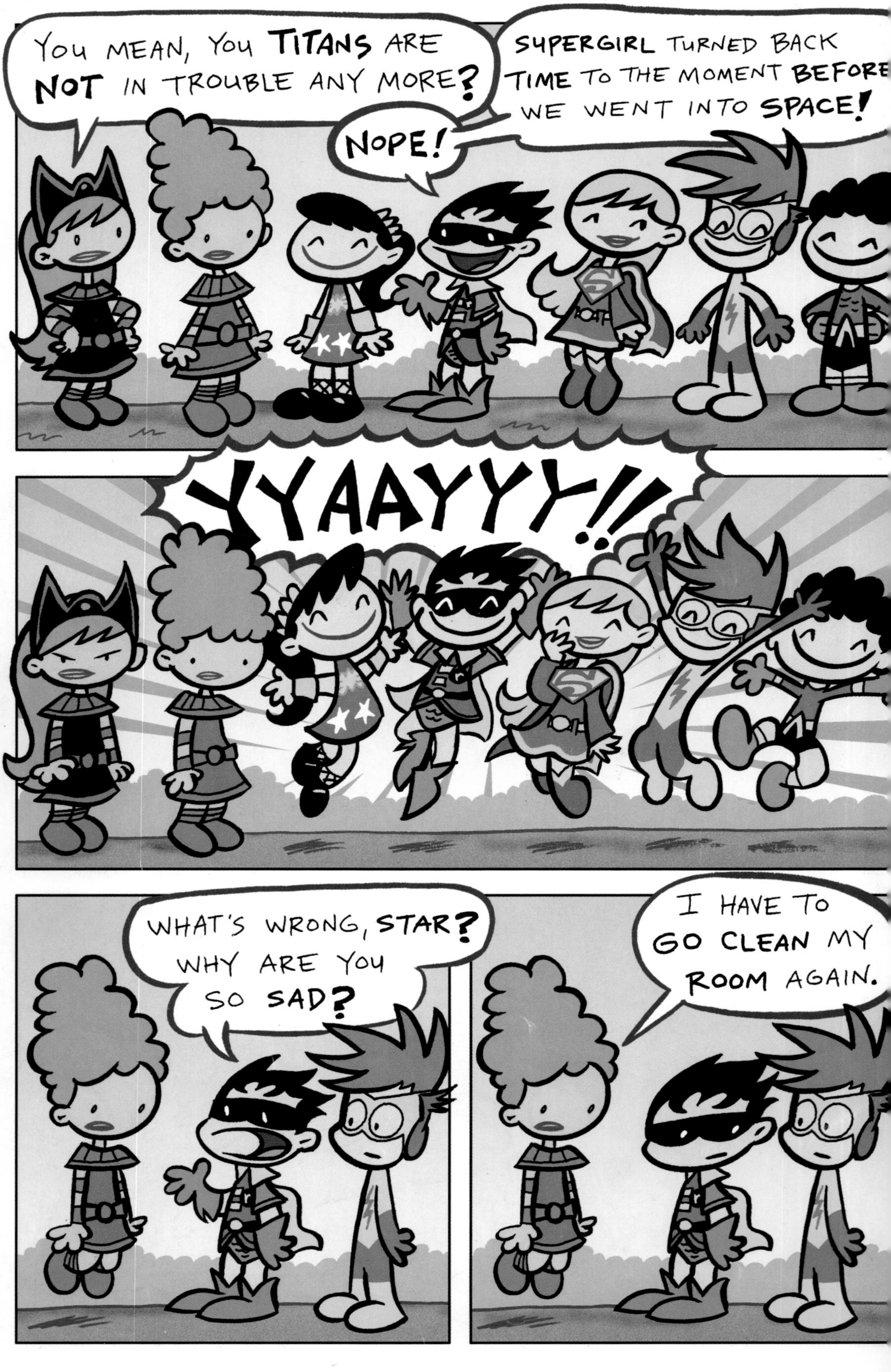
YOU MEAN, YOU TITANS ARE NOT IN TROUBLE ANY MORE?
NOPE!
SUPERGIRL TURNED BACK TIME TO THE MOMENT BEFORE WE WENT INTO SPACE!
YYAAYYY!!
WHAT'S WRONG, STAR? WHY ARE YOU SO SAD?
I HAVE TO GO CLEAN MY ROOM AGAIN.

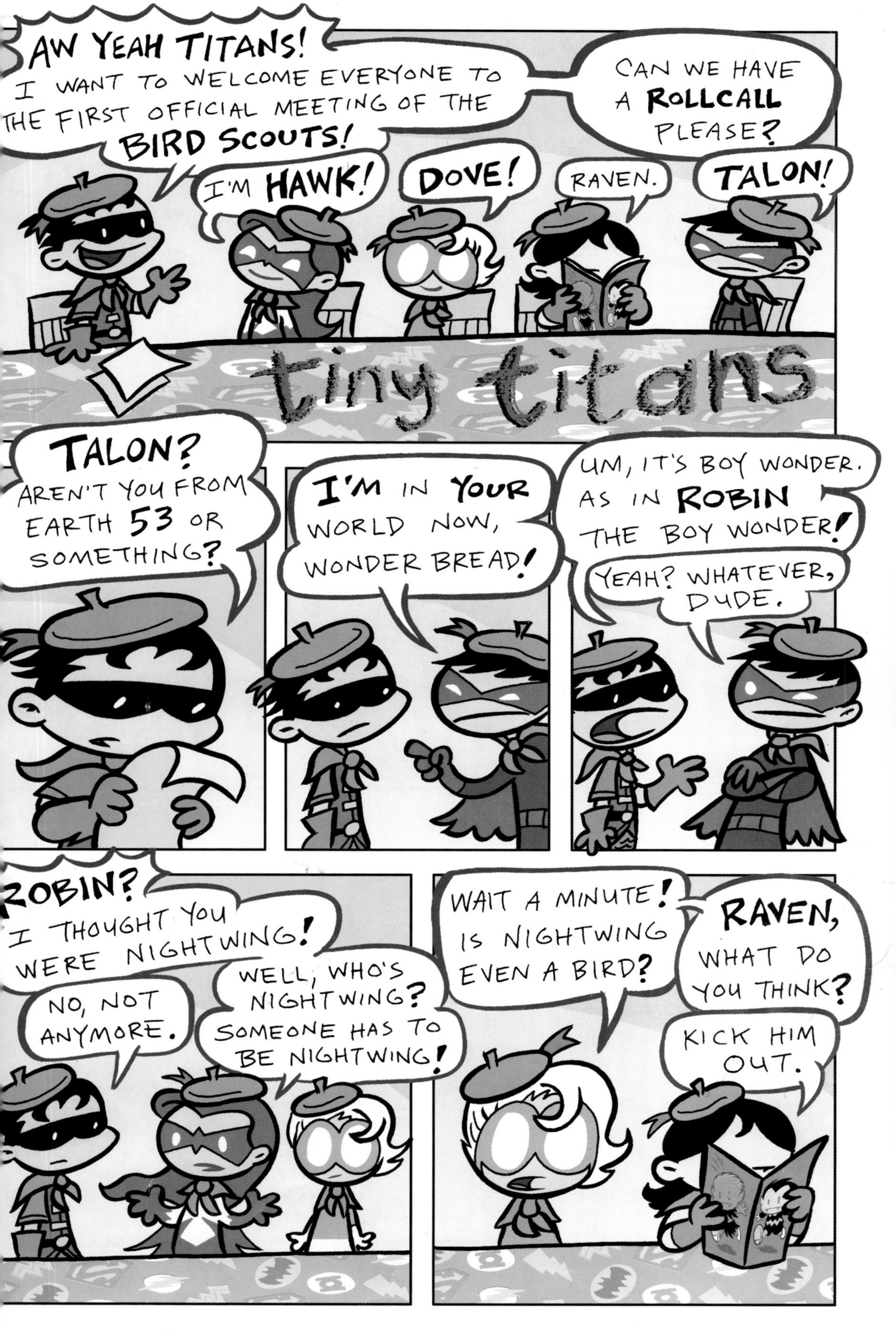
AW YEAH TITANS! I WANT TO WELCOME EVERYONE TO THE FIRST OFFICIAL MEETING OF THE BIRD SCOUTS!
CAN WE HAVE A ROLLCALL PLEASE?
I'M HAWK!
DOVE!
RAVEN.
TALON!
tiny titans
TALON? AREN'T YOU FROM EARTH 53 OR SOMETHING?
I'M IN YOUR WORLD NOW, WONDER BREAD!
UM, IT'S BOY WONDER. AS IN ROBIN THE BOY WONDER!
YEAH? WHATEVER, DUDE.
ROBIN? I THOUGHT YOU WERE NIGHTWING!
NO, NOT ANYMORE.
WELL, WHO'S NIGHTWING? SOMEONE HAS TO BE NIGHTWING!
WAIT A MINUTE! IS NIGHTWING EVEN A BIRD?
RAVEN, WHAT DO YOU THINK?
KICK HIM OUT.

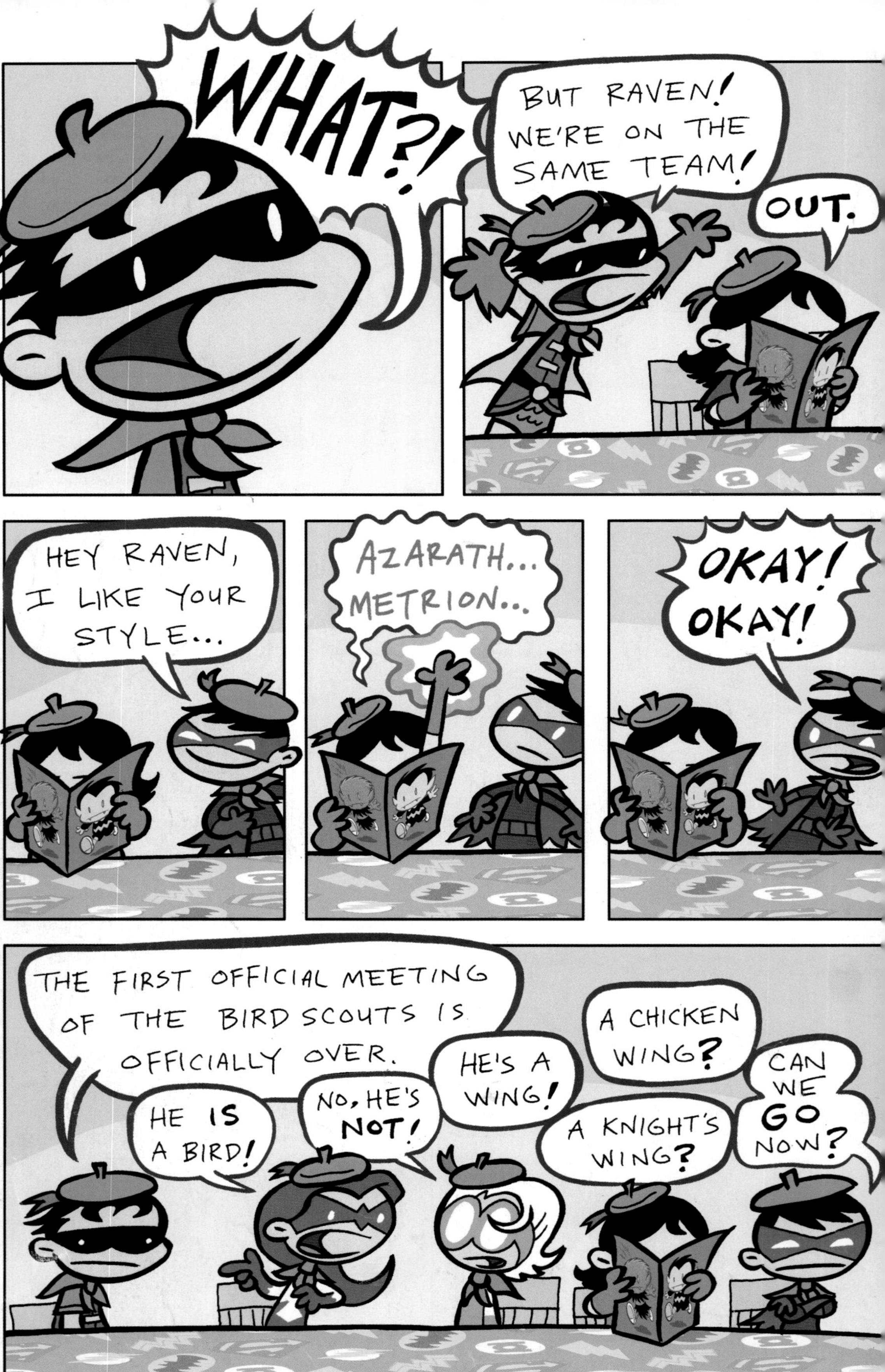
WHAT?!
BUT RAVEN! WE'RE ON THE SAME TEAM!
OUT.
HEY RAVEN, I LIKE YOUR STYLE...
AZARATH... METRION...
OKAY! OKAY!
THE FIRST OFFICIAL MEETING OF THE BIRD SCOUTS IS OFFICIALLY OVER.
HE **IS** A BIRD!
NO, HE'S **NOT**!
HE'S A WING!
A CHICKEN WING?
A KNIGHT'S WING?
CAN WE **GO** NOW?

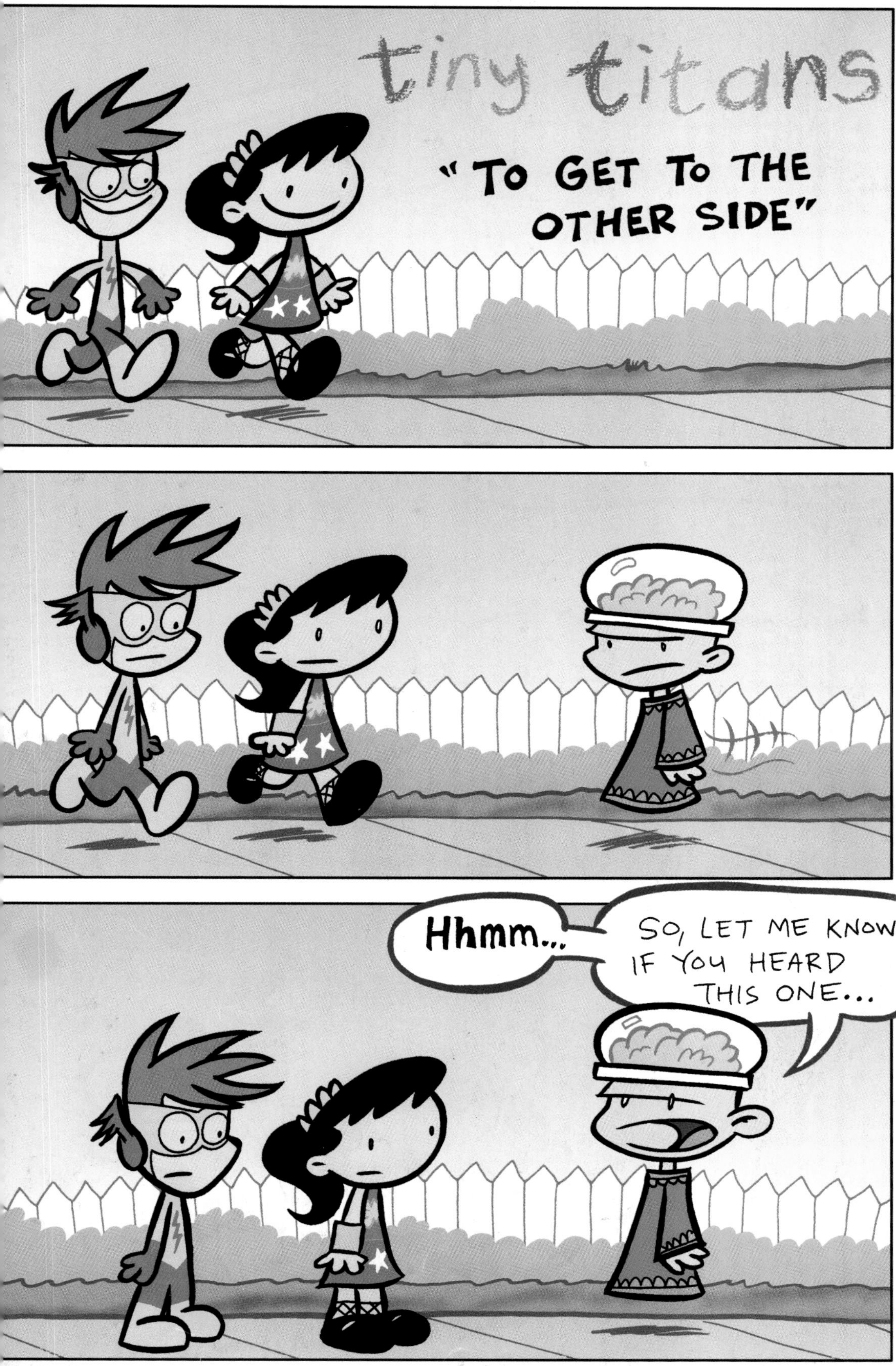
tiny titans
"TO GET TO THE OTHER SIDE"
Hhmm...
SO, LET ME KNOW IF YOU HEARD THIS ONE...

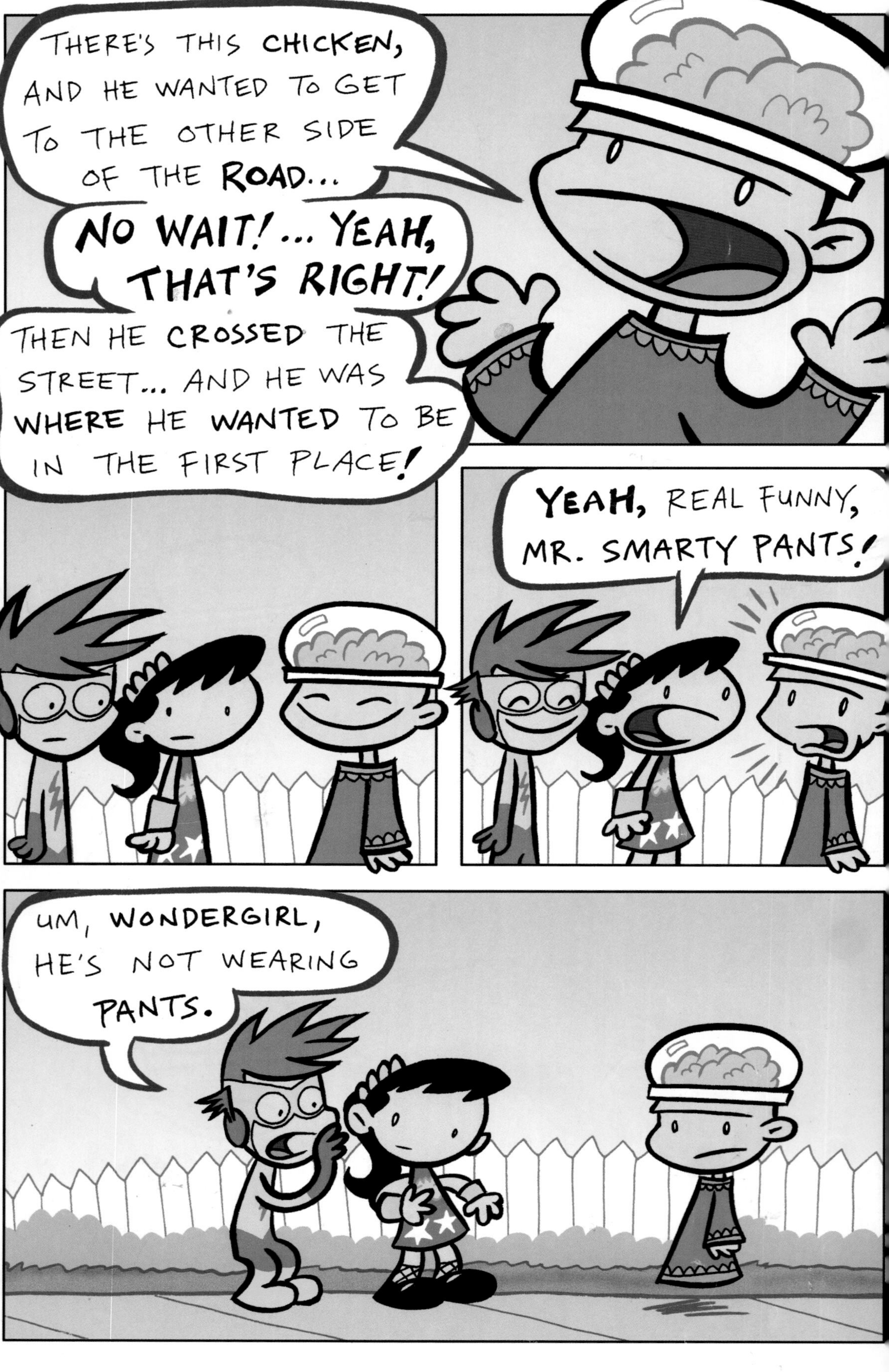
THERE'S THIS CHICKEN, AND HE WANTED TO GET TO THE OTHER SIDE OF THE ROAD...
NO WAIT! ... YEAH, THAT'S RIGHT!
THEN HE CROSSED THE STREET... AND HE WAS WHERE HE WANTED TO BE IN THE FIRST PLACE!
YEAH, REAL FUNNY, MR. SMARTY PANTS!
UM, WONDERGIRL, HE'S NOT WEARING PANTS.

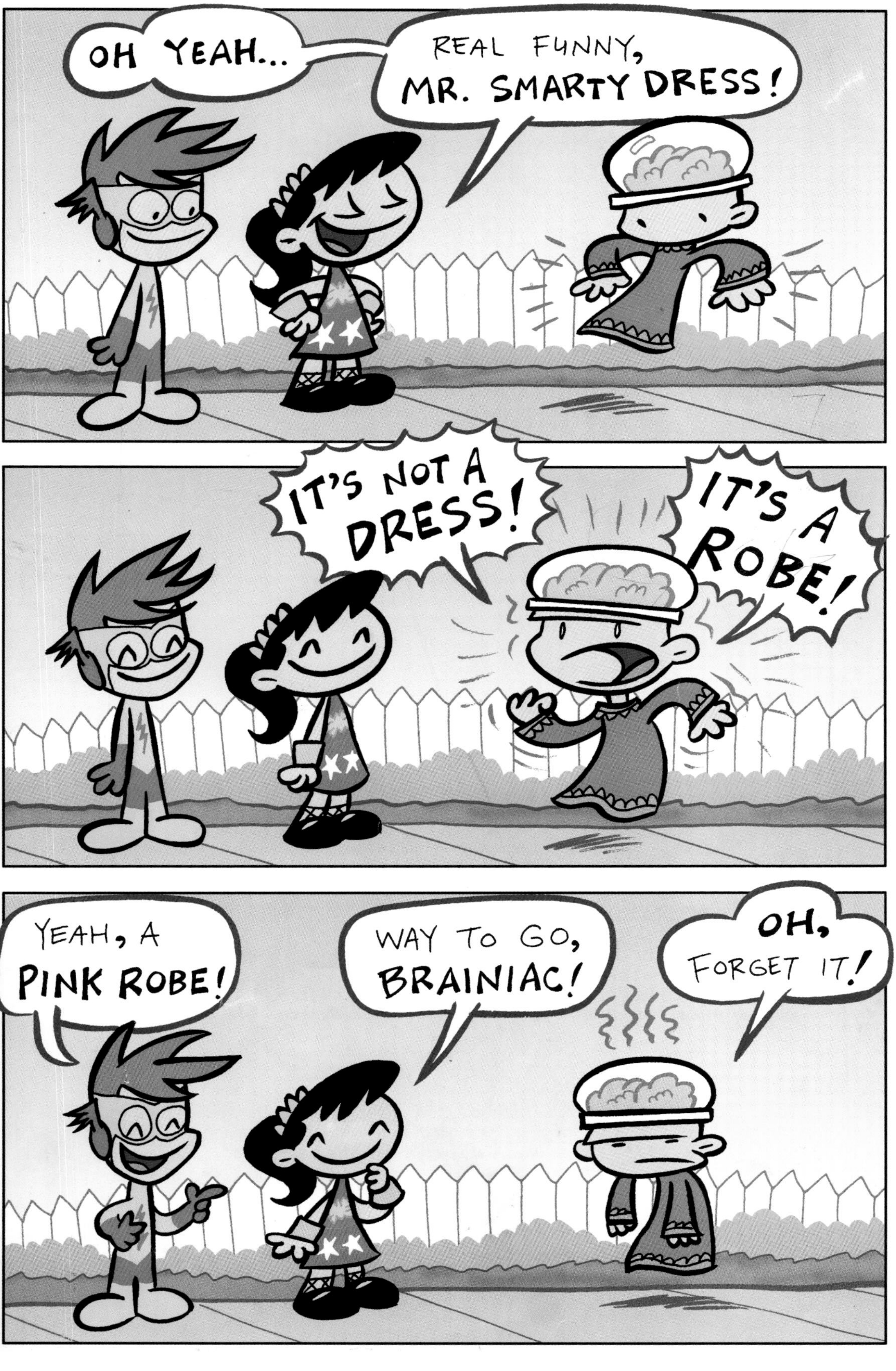
OH YEAH...
REAL FUNNY, MR. SMARTY DRESS!
IT'S NOT A DRESS!
IT'S A ROBE!
YEAH, A PINK ROBE!
WAY TO GO, BRAINIAC!
OH, FORGET IT!

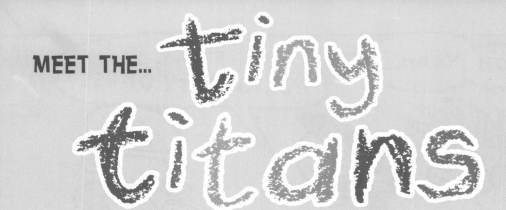

MEET THE... tiny titans

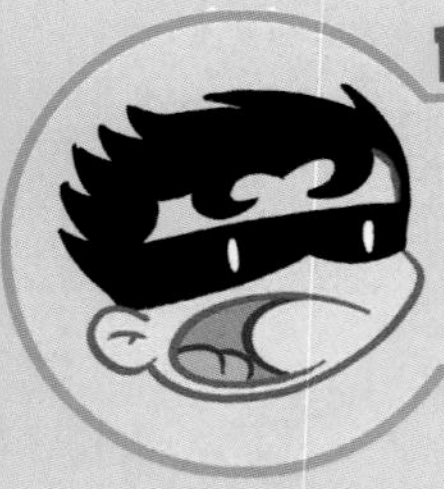

ROBIN

(Dick Grayson)- The brave and serious leader of the Tiny Titans. Although he is the original Robin, he is very moody and has to share his room with his brothers, the other Robins. Also, he has secret crushes for Starfire and Barbara Gordon.

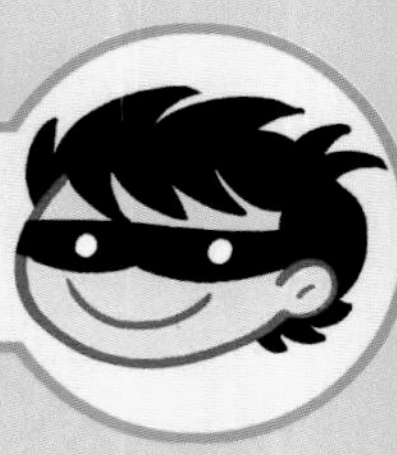

JASON TODDLER

The youngest of the three Robins. Too young to go to school, Jason is always in a happy mood and has a care-free style. He's all about smiling and having fun.

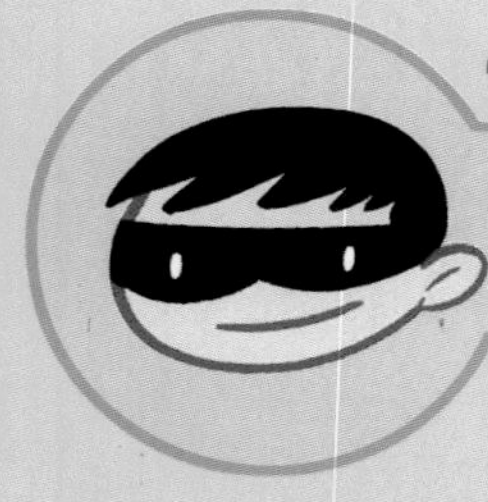

TIM DRAKE

The cool Robin. Tim wants to stand out from his brothers by wearing his own unique Robin costume. He's very laid back and easy going indeed.

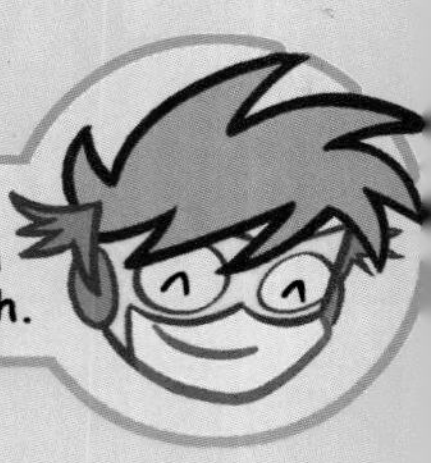

KID FLASH

The super speedster and fasted kid in the school. Quick witted and eats lots for lunch because of his high metabolism. Too much candy will cause major sugar rush.

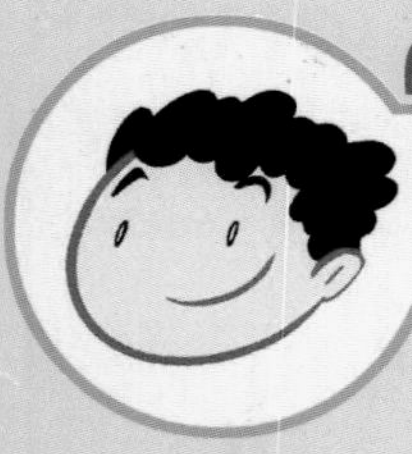

AQUALAD

The little boy from the ocean. Has a pet fish named Fluffy. Aqualad can communicate with all forms of sea life, even the pet hamster in their classroom.

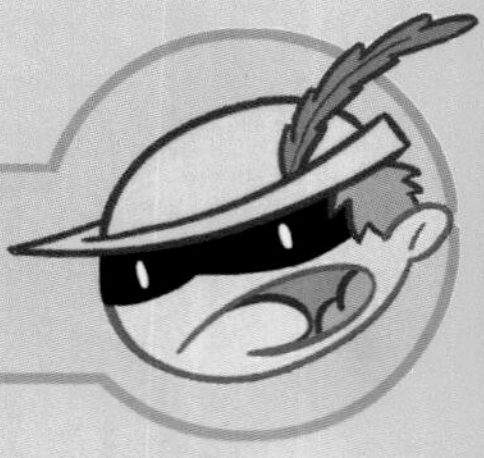

SPEEDY

Quiet and cool, he is the boy with the trick arrows. He's good at anything that requires aiming. Also, he's Kid Flash's best friend.

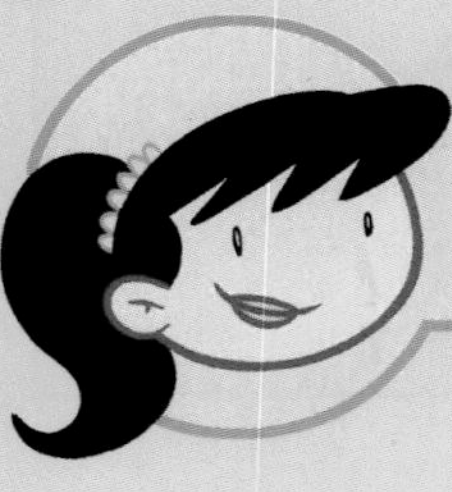

WONDER GIRL

(Donna) Raised by amazons. She's strong and cute. Never lie to her, she has a magical jump rope which makes people tell the truth. Very skeptic.

RAVEN

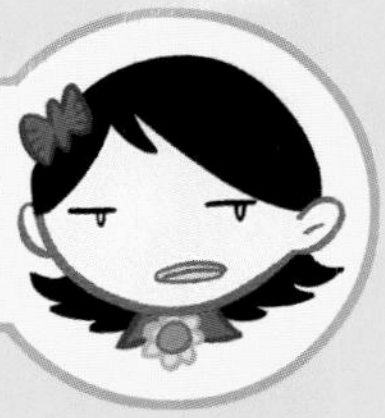

The quiet and mysterious little girl. She really likes to experiment with dark magic, which usually turn into bad practical jokes. Mr. Trigon, the substitute teacher is her father.

CYBORG

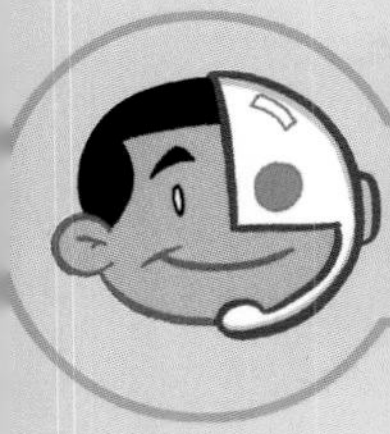

Half boy, half robot. Cyborg is always tinkering with mechanical gadgets, often turning them into something else. His battle cry "BOO-YA!" has earned him the nickname, "Big Boo-Ya".

BEAST BOY

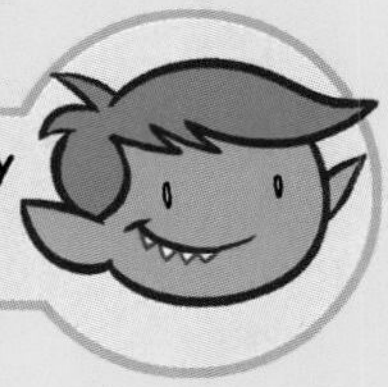

The green little boy who can change into any animal he desires. He's a prankster and loves comics. Has a crush on Terra.

STARFIRE

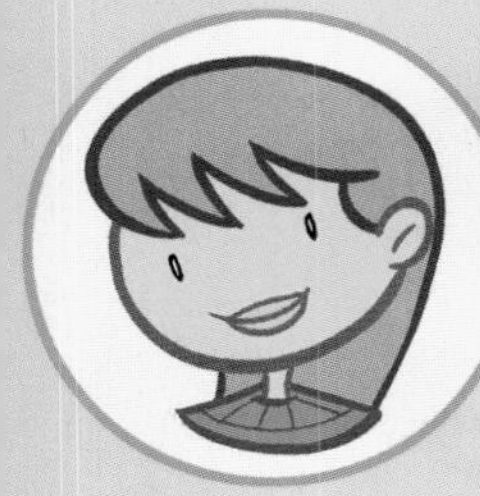

She's an alien princess. Very naïve and free spirited and finds the good in others. Has a crush on Robin and thinks he's cute, but so do all the other girls.

KID DEVIL

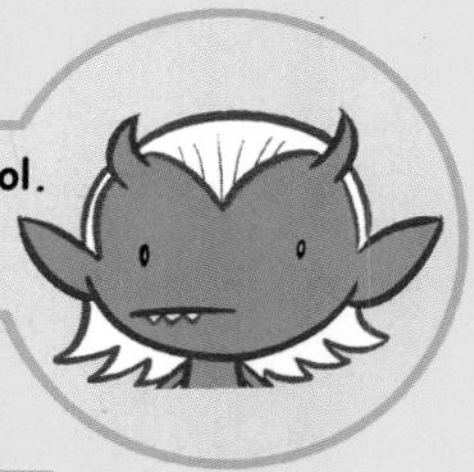

One of the younger Tiny Titans, still too young for school. Cannot talk but can breathe fire, usually while coughing or sneezing or hiccupping.

ROSE & JERICHO

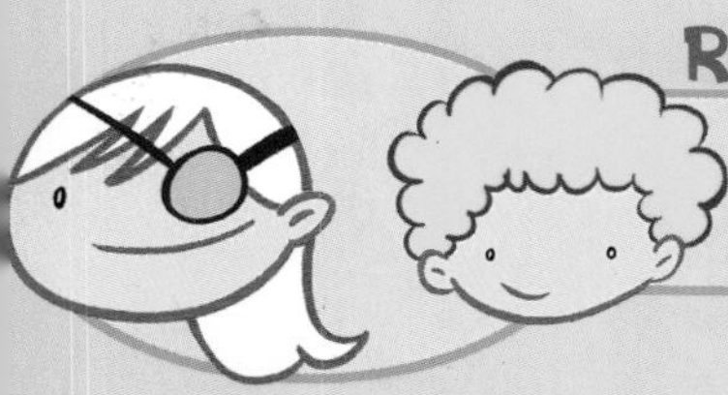

Principal Slade's kids. Rose is the older and tougher "Tom-Boy" of the two. Jericho can't speak, but can take over your mind if you look into his eyes.

MISS MARTIAN

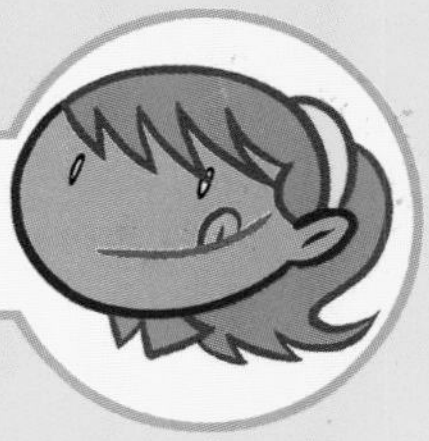

A shape shifting little girl alien from Mars who is still too young to go to school. She is often mistaken for Beast Boy's little sister.

TERRA

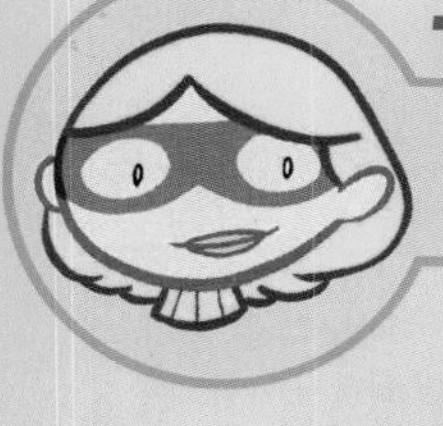

The sometimes hated little girl who likes to throw rocks. Principal Slade's teacher's pet. She thinks Beast Boy is a weirdo.

CASSIE

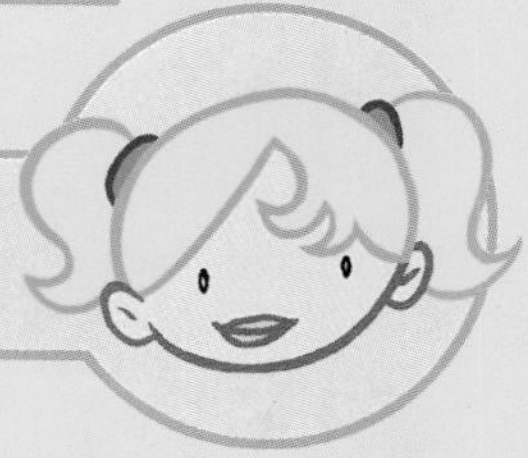

Wonder Girl's rich cousin from the big city. Cassie's really into fashion and is hip to all the latest trends in POP culture.

BUMBLE BEE

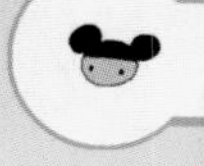

The tiniest of the Tiny Titans.
BB buzzes and packs a mighty stinger.

Creators

Art Baltazar is a cartoonist machine from the heart of Chicago! He defines cartoons and comics not only as an art style, but as a way of life. Currently, Art is the creative force behind *The New York Times* best-selling, Eisner Award-winning, DC Comics series Tiny Titans, and the co-writer for Billy Batson and the Magic of SHAZAM! and co-creator of Superman Family Adventures. Art is living the dream! He draws comics and never has to leave the house. He lives with his lovely wife, Rose, big boy Sonny, little boy Gordon, and little girl Audrey. Right on!

ART BALTAZAR

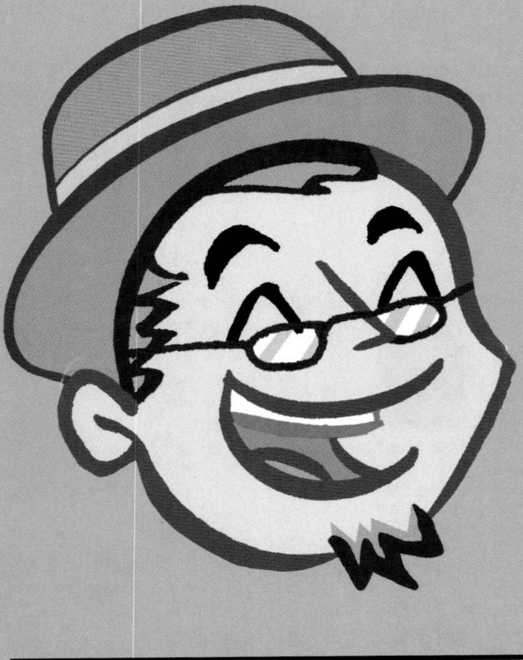

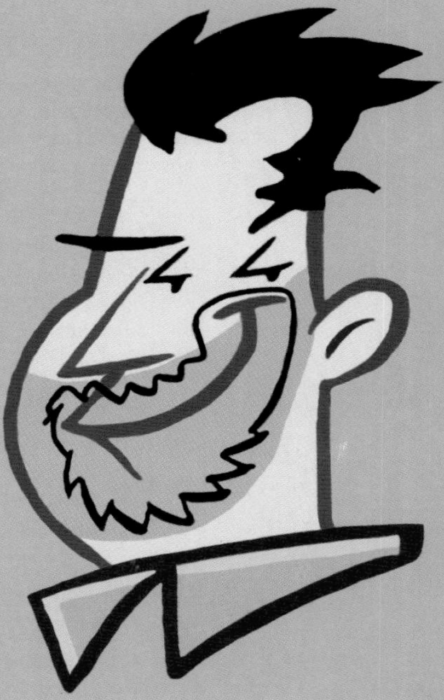

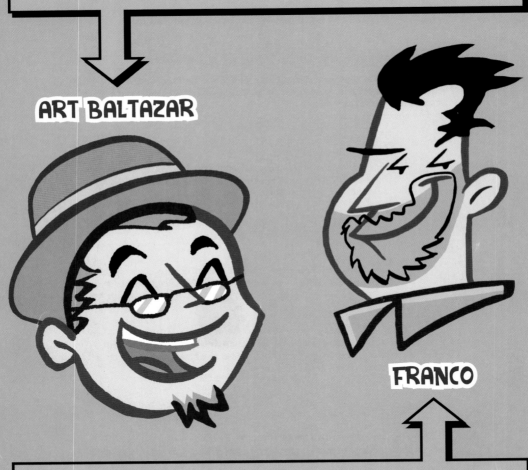

FRANCO

Bronx, New York born writer and artist Franco Aureliani has been drawing comics since he could hold a crayon. Currently residing in upstate New York with his wife, Ivette, and son, Nicolas, Franco spends most of his days in a Batcave-like studio where he produces DC's Tiny Titans comics. In 1995, Franco founded Blindwolf Studios, an independent art studio where he and fellow creators can create children's comics. Franco is the creator, artist, and writer of Weirdsville, L'il Creeps, and Eagle All Star, as well as the co-creator and writer of Patrick the Wolf Boy. When he's not writing and drawing, Franco also teaches high school art.

Glossary

BONUS [BOH-nuhss] – a good thing that is more than you expected

GROUNDED [GROUN-did] – not allowed to take part in some usual activities

OFFICIAL [uh-FISH-uhl] – something approved by someone in authority

PREPARE [pri-PAIR] – to get ready

REVERSE [ri-VURSS] – to change to the opposite direction

TAKEOFF [TAYK-awf] – the beginning of a flight, when an aircraft leaves the ground

TALON [TAL-uhn] – a sharp claw of a bird, such as an eagle, a hawk, or a falcon

Action Accessories

Speedy

BOW AND ARROW

Robin

CAPE

Terra

ROCKS

Aqualad

FLUFFY

Wonder Girl

MAGIC JUMP ROPE

Visual Questions & Prompts

1. WHAT DOES SUPERGIRL DO TO TURN BACK TIME SO THE TITANS DON'T GET GROUNDED? IS THIS A GOOD OR BAD THING? HOW SO?

1
SPIN
REVERSE
WHOOSH
AXIS
REVERSE
REVERSE
SPIN
WHOOSH

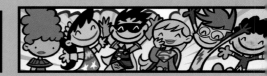

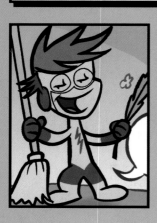

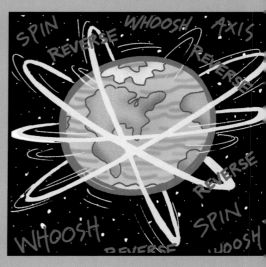

2. HOW ARE THE TINY TITANS ABLE TO GET STAR'S ROOM CLEAN SO FAST? WHY IS KID FLASH THE BEST ONE FOR THE JOB?

2
CLEAN
FAST
SWEEP
FAST

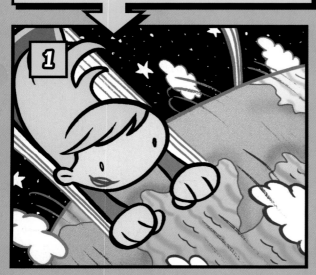

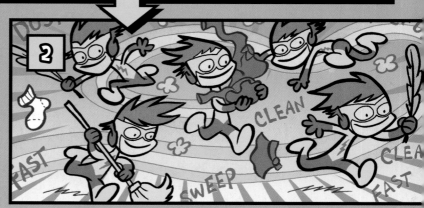

3. IN COMICS, CHARACTERS' FACIAL EXPRESSIONS OFTEN TELL YOU WHAT THEY'RE FEELING. WHAT CAN YOU TELL ABOUT HOW THE TINY TITANS FEEL BASED ON THE PANEL?

YEAH, OKAY!
3

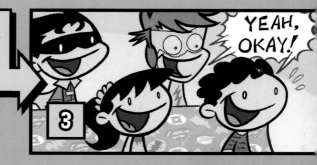

4. WHAT DO YOU THINK IS GOING ON IN THE PANEL BELOW? HOW CAN YOU TELL? WRITE 2-3 SENTENCES TO EXPLAIN YOUR ANSWER.

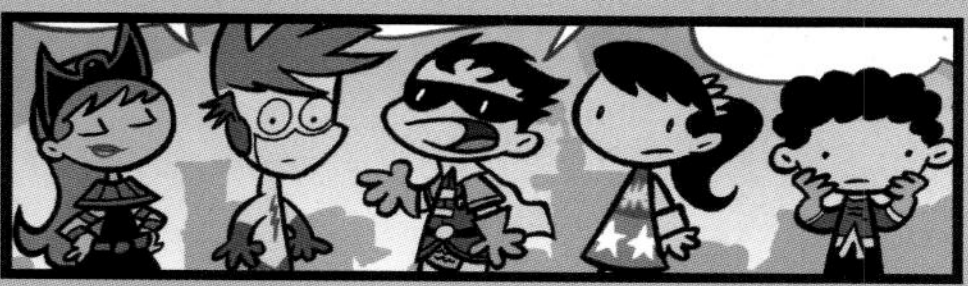

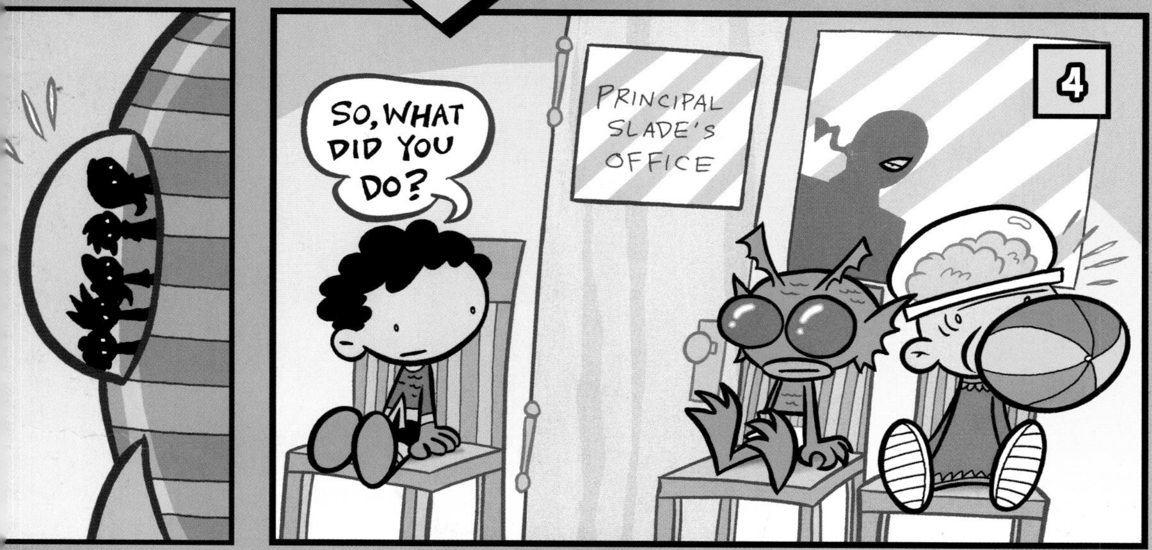
4
SO, WHAT DID YOU DO?
PRINCIPAL SLADE'S OFFICE

5. WHAT DO THE FOLLOWING PANELS TELL YOU ABOUT HOW BRAINIAC FEELS ABOUT HIS NAME? WRITE 2-3 SENTENCES EXPLAINING YOUR ANSWER.

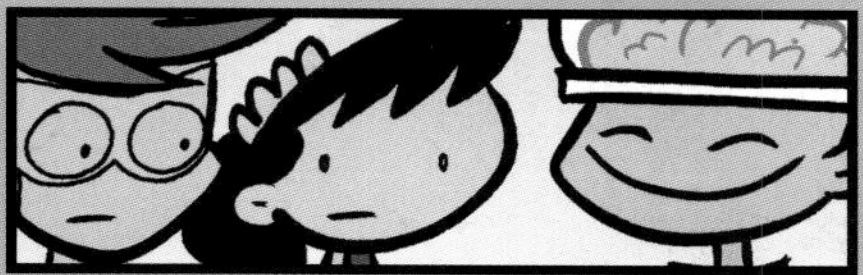

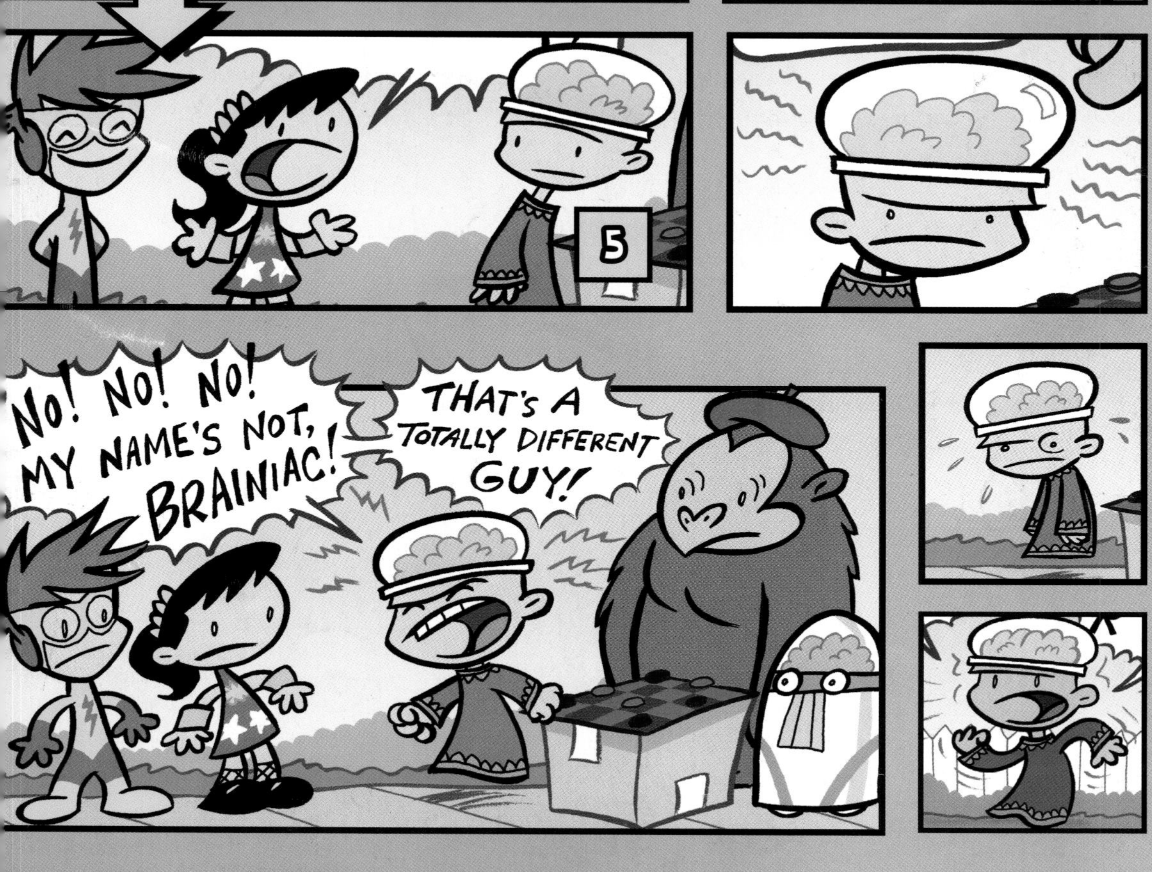
5
NO! NO! NO! MY NAME'S NOT, BRAINIAC!
THAT'S A TOTALLY DIFFERENT GUY!

tiny titans

DC COMICS
tiny titans
Meet Tiny Titans East!
By Eisner Winners Art Baltazar & Franco
WHAT'S GOING ON?
I'M NOT SURE. IS IT ROBIN OR NIGHTWING?

tiny titans
Welcome to the Treehouse
AW YEAH, TITANS!
titans
AW YEAH, TITANS!
By Eisner Winners Art Baltazar & Franco

tiny titans
DUDE, RELAX. IN SPACE, NO ONE CAN HEAR YOU SCREAM.
AAAHH!
THAT'S FUNNY, IT'S PRETTY LOUD IN THIS COCKPIT!
By Eisner Winners Art Baltazar & Franco
Titans in Space

tiny titans
SIDEKICK CITY ELEMENTARY
AW YEAH, TITANS! WHAT GRADE DID YOU GET IN MATH?
I GOT AN "A"!
I GOT A "C".
I GOT A ROCK.
By Eisner Winners Art Baltazar & Franco
Report Card Pickup!

tiny titans
By Eisner Winners Art Baltazar & Franco
Sidekick City Elementary

tiny titans
vs. the Fearsome Five
By Eisner Winners Art Baltazar & Franco

tiny titans
AND I THOUGHT THE BATS WERE A PROBLEM!
By Eisner Winners Art Baltazar & Franco
Penguins in the Batcave!

tiny titans
Enter: Nightwing!
ROBIN, YOUR NEW COSTUME'S AWESOME!
AW YEAH! THIS DANCE PARTY ROCKS!
By Eisner Winners Art Baltazar & Franco

FIND COOL WEBSITES AND MORE BOOKS LIKE THIS ONE AT WWW.FACTHOUND.COM.
JUST TYPE IN THE BOOK ID: 978-1-4342-4698-1

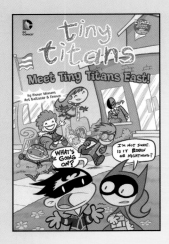

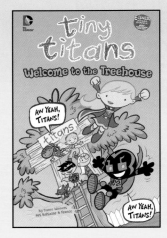

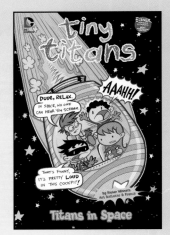

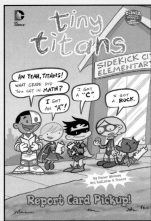

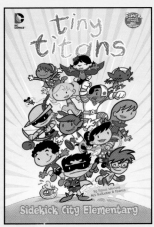

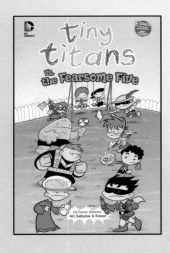

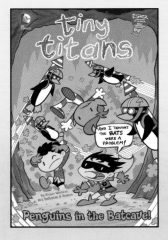

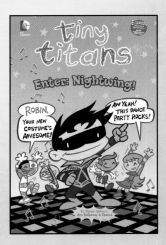